DON'T TELL THE NAZIS

Also by Marsha Forchuk Skrypuch

Making Bombs for Hitler
The War Below
Stolen Girl

TELL THE NAZIS

A novel by
MARSHA FORCHUK SKRYPUCH

SCHOLASTIC PRESS | NEW YORK

THIS NOVEL IS DEDICATED TO KRYSTIA, WHOSE BRAVERY TAKES MY BREATH AWAY.
–M.S.

All rights reserved. Published by Scholastic Press, an imprint of Scholastic Inc., *Publishers since 1920*. SCHOLASTIC, SCHOLASTIC PRESS, and associated logos are trademarks and/or registered trademarks of Scholastic Inc.

First published in Canada as *Don't Tell the Enemy* by Scholastic Canada Ltd., 604 King Street West, Toronto, Ontario M5V 1E1, Canada

The publisher does not have any control over and does not assume any responsibility for author or third-party websites or their content.

Library of Congress Cataloging-in-Publication Data available

ISBN 978-1-338-31053-5

10 9 8 7 6 5 4 3 2 1   19 20 21 22 23

Printed in the U.S.A.   23

First American edition, December 2019

Book design by Yaffa Jaskoll

CHAPTER ONE
THE END OF THEM

June 28, 1941, Viteretz, Ukraine

I huddled close to my sister under the comforter and prayed that we'd live through the night. At any moment the door might burst open and we could be dragged from our beds.

Another gunshot. Running footsteps. Screams.

A low, growling *boom*.

The bedroom flashed bright for one brief moment and I saw the terror on Mama's face as she pointed the pistol toward the closed door. The room plunged back into darkness.

Silence. Moments passed.

"Krystia and Maria," whispered Mama, "try to sleep. Maybe the Soviets will be gone by morning."

How I longed to get back to what it was like before the war—with enough food to eat and without having to walk with my eyes cast to the ground, afraid to speak to a friend for fear of being arrested.

I lay back down on my pillow, listening for the next volley of gunfire.

We had all heard that the friendship between the Germans and Soviets had fallen apart, and that the Germans were pushing out the Soviets. But as that happened, the Soviets were like angry bees, attacking us *civilians* and stealing all they could as they fled.

As the minutes ticked by, Mama and Maria both drifted into sleep, and their rhythmic breathing muffled the sound of explosions—more distant now—but I could not relax. I tried to breathe slowly to lull myself to sleep.

A low squeak of rusted hinges.

I bolted up. It sounded like someone opening the door of the cowshed alongside the house. I climbed out of bed, crept to the main room, and pressed my ear against the wall.

A faint *thump* and then the crunch of straw. Someone was definitely in our hayloft. Was it someone fleeing from the Soviets? If we were caught hiding a runaway, they'd punish us.

If I were brave, I'd go there now and find out who it was, but I was too frightened to do that. Instead, I got back into bed and closed my eyes, praying that whoever was hiding in the shed would be gone by morning. I hoped Mama wouldn't wake up and investigate the noise. What if the runaway got scared and shot her? With Tato already dead, I couldn't bear the thought of losing Mama too. I forced myself to slowly breathe in and out, and prayed that the runaway would leave before we had to figure out what to do.

Somehow, I slept.

Beams of daylight through the bedroom window woke me. All was silent. Mama slept, her pistol resting on her chest with one hand flopped on top of it. Even though I didn't feel all that brave, I was the older daughter, so it was my responsibility to protect what was left of our family. I got out of bed, careful not to wake Maria, and slid the pistol out from under Mama's hand. I put it into the pocket of my nightgown, then tiptoed to the big room.

With my ear against the wall, I listened, but now the only sound from the cowshed was Krasa's familiar breathing. I peeked out at the road from behind the curtains. No soldiers. I grabbed the milking pail, opened the front door, and stepped out.

CHAPTER TWO
IN THE LOFT

It was almost too quiet. Across the road, the Segals' house was dark. Beside it, St. Mary's Ukrainian Catholic Church stood boarded up and silent, but there was a flicker of a curtain from the window of Father Andrij's house just beside it. Was his wife checking to see if it was safe to go out yet?

I stepped into the shed and put the pail down, then held the pistol with both hands and twirled around. No one was there—except for Krasa—and she was looking spooked. She stomped one hoof as if she were agitated from last night's explosions and gunfire. Any intruder would have made it that much worse.

I held the gun behind my back and put my face up to hers. "Shhh," I whispered, rubbing the bridge of her nose.

I climbed the wooden rungs to the loft, holding the gun in one hand. When my head was just below the hole in the floor, I counted to three and burst up, trying to steady the pistol with one hand. "Don't move!"

A scrabbling noise from the far corner. I pointed the pistol.

"Krystia! Put the gun down, it's me."

"Josip?" I climbed up the rest of the way. My cousin sat cross-legged in a nest of straw beside our stash of goods from Auntie Stefa in Toronto. Josip looked exhausted.

"The Soviet secret police nearly caught me last night."

"Why would they be after *you*?" I asked.

"The NKVD are always after someone. Right now they seem to be rounding up educated Ukrainians."

"Where's Borys?" I asked. My cousins were usually inseparable.

"There's a good place in the forest. A lot of us have taken refuge there. I'm hoping Borys found it."

"Is that where you'll hide too?"

He shook his head. "The NKVD could follow me there."

"You can stay here . . ."

"That would put *you* in danger."

"But where will you go?"

He shrugged. "I'll have to see."

I crawled over to where Josip sat and rested my head on his shoulder. "I've really missed you since you've been off to university."

"I miss you and Maria too," he said.

"Can I visit you in Lviv after the Soviets leave?"

"I'd like that," he said. "And I'm hoping that you can attend university yourself one day."

"Maria too?"

"Of course." He rested his hand on top of mine and I noticed his familiar crooked baby finger. Once, when we had been playing hide-and-seek, he'd got his finger caught in a door (it wasn't my fault) and it ended up healing with a permanent bend.

"Why don't you slip into the house by the bedroom window and Mama will make you breakfast?"

"That's too dangerous, Krystia—for you and for me," said Josip. "And I need to be on my way."

"What about some milk from Krasa, then?" I asked.

"That sounds good," said Josip. "And it will be quick."

He followed me down the ladder and stood in the corner as I milked Krasa. When I was finished, he held the heavy pail to his lips and swallowed a few gulps.

"Go about your business as if I'm not here," he told me, wiping his mouth with the back of his hand.

I leaned into him and rested my head on his shoulder. "Stay safe, Cousin. You and Borys both."

He kissed the top of my head. "You too, Cousin."

We stood like that for a full minute before he stepped away. "Get going, Krystia."

I slid the pistol into my pocket and blew Josip one last kiss, then hefted the bucket and walked back to the house.

Mama was wiping down the wooden stove with a soapy rag. She paused mid-swipe as I set the bucket on the table. "Why did you do the milking in your nightgown?" she asked me. "And why did you take my pistol?"

I gave Mama back the gun and told her about Josip. She inhaled sharply.

The bedroom door creaked open and Maria walked out, wearing the shabbier of our shared outfits. "I almost wore the good clothing, seeing as it was lying there, tempting me. But I decided that it wouldn't be fair," she said.

To save arguments, the two of us had long ago agreed that the first one to rise got to wear the best skirt and blouse.

"Now, what's this about Josip?" asked Maria.

"NKVD," said Mama. "He's in our shed."

Maria's face paled. "Doesn't he know he's putting us in danger?"

I kept my mouth shut, but I could feel the anger boiling inside. Why did Maria think only of *our* safety?

"Don't you even *care* about Josip?" I asked. So much for keeping my mouth shut.

Mama looked from me to Maria. "Enough," she said. "Krystia, go get dressed."

"But . . ."

"Go."

I felt like stomping to the bedroom, but I knew Mama wouldn't put up with that either, so with all the dignity I could muster, I *walked* to the bedroom to change.

As soon as I was there, my anger lightened. How could I be angry with my little sister when she had left me the best skirt and blouse? Yes, we had a deal, but Maria could have argued that I'd forfeited the good clothes by not getting dressed when I got up. It was sweet that she hadn't done that. And I didn't mind that Maria wore the shoes, because they pinched my heels.

By the time I stepped back into the main room, Maria had fed our two chickens and had already left to get water. There were chores to do, whether there were still NKVD about or not.

I went back to the shed, hoping Josip was still there, but he had left. "Josip, dear Josip," I whispered under my breath. "Be safe, be brave."

I looped a rope around Krasa's neck and led her outside. Taking her to pasture should have been a job shared by Maria and me, but Maria was terrified to take the long walk on her own. Normally, I didn't mind, as it was

pleasant to spend time with Krasa and it was certainly easier than lugging endless buckets of water, but if there were
still NKVD about, I was sure to run into them. There was
no way out of this chore, though, because if I didn't take
Krasa to pasture, her milk would dry up, and *then* where
would we be?

When I looked toward town, all I saw was Maria waiting in line at the pump, chatting with Nathan Segal. He
was eleven, but he had been sweet on my sister for as long
as I could remember.

The Zhuks next door still had their house closed up
tight. Mr. Zhuk, a bookkeeper, had been deported to a
Siberian slave camp more than a year ago, so it was only
his wife, Valentina, and her son, Petro, living there now. I
turned and stood on tiptoe to look toward the outskirts of
town—and again, no people were out except for me,
Maria, and Nathan.

Low in the sky, a German airplane—distinctive with
its cross and swastika—growled above us, making Krasa
tremble. I had seen dozens of these in the last two days, all
heading toward Lviv. I hoped the Germans would banish
the Soviets once and for all.

We started on our two-kilometer walk to the pasture
and I kept my eyes to the ground and my ears tuned for
unusual sounds. We passed the Kitais' house, beside

9

ours—but it was also dark and silent. Mr. Kitai ran a school supply store and Mina Kitai was a doctor—everyone called her Doctor Mina. I imagined my classmate Dolik still sound asleep in his soft, warm bed. His little brother, Leon, too.

Mama cleaned for Doctor Mina. The Kitais were well-to-do enough that they could have been deported to Siberia as "bourgeois," but Doctor Mina took on some of the Soviet officers as her patients. Mama just had to be careful to avoid them when she went in to clean, though, because if the Soviets thought Doctor Mina had a servant, that could still get her deported.

I could feel my face getting hot at the thought of my mother working as a servant to my classmate. But Doctor Mina was so kind, just like her husband. More than once he had given us pencils and paper for school at no charge. And Doctor Mina had looked after Tato when he was dying of lung cancer. She'd been at our house nearly every day during that awful time.

I continued down the road, passing many empty houses, thinking of all the changes in the two years of Soviet occupation. Of the four thousand or so people who had lived in Viteretz before the war, only eight hundred were Ukrainians, with about sixteen hundred Poles, and the same number of Jews. When the Polish government had held power, they put a quota on Ukrainians in professions and trades, so most couldn't afford to live in town. They could only be farmers. On our entire long street of St. Olha—Karl Marx Street now, according to the Soviets— we had just four Ukrainian families: us, Uncle Roman and Auntie Iryna Fediuk (because of our blacksmith shop), the Zhuk family, and Father Andrij and his wife, Anya.

The surrounding farmlands were the opposite—mostly poor Ukrainian farmers with just a few Polish and Jewish families mixed in. At the beginning of the occupation, the Soviets were kind to the poor, but they terrorized the wealthy, meaning mostly Poles. Many were killed or deported to slave camps in Siberia. Now, it seemed, they were turning on the Ukrainians.

All at once I heard footsteps behind me. My heart raced. But it was just Uncle Roman, my father's brother.

He stepped in beside me, mopping his brow with his yellow handkerchief. "Krystia, my slow niece," he said. "It looks like we're both late this morning. It took a long time to get Lysa out of her stall."

I reached over and patted her nose, then lowered my voice. "Josip was hiding in our shed this morning, but now he's gone."

"Ah," Uncle Roman said. "Thank the Virgin Mary that my son is safe. Did he have any news of Borys?"

"Hiding in the forest from the Soviets, Josip thinks."

Uncle Roman's shoulders relaxed.

When Borys and Josip had lived at home, they would alternate taking Lysa to their pasture and we often walked together. Since they'd gone to university, it had fallen to Uncle Roman to walk the cow himself. He didn't seem to mind, though. It gave him a break from the blacksmith shop, and he'd often meet his friends and they'd chat as their cows munched the grass.

Uncle Roman's pasture was just beyond mine. Before he took Lysa there, he gave me a stern look. "Wait for me when Krasa is finished grazing so we can walk back to town together. It's not safe with the soldiers about."

"Thanks, Uncle," I said, standing on my toes and kissing him on his cheek.

I guided Krasa through the bushes and undid her rope so she could graze while I picked raspberries.

I should have brought a pail, but between Josip and all the shooting last night, I had forgotten. At least my apron had deep pockets. I reached through the thorny bushes to get to the ripest berries.

Just then I heard low grinding screeches coming from the road. Artem Bronsek was guiding a slope-backed horse as it pulled a cart filled with a variety of goods that looked like they'd been stolen from different houses and stores.

His wife, Olga, sat on the bench beside him, and their daughter, Sonia, sat perched on a carved box as she steadied a painting of a long-dead princess on her knee.

I knew exactly where that painting had been stolen from—the Tarnowsky house in our town square. Mama used to clean that house too, before the war.

Next, two Soviet trucks rumbled past. One was piled high with stolen goods; the other carried half a dozen soldiers clutching rifles. I let the branches close and kept still, counting the long seconds it took for the trucks to pass.

A minute later, three loud gunshots erupted in rapid succession. Even as they fled, the Soviets wanted to scare us.

CHAPTER THREE
BLOOD AND RASPBERRIES

My pockets bulged with raspberries and Krasa had long finished grazing, but Uncle Roman still hadn't come back. While I was anxious to get home, he had told me to wait, so I sat down on a rock and chewed on a blade of grass. Krasa ambled over and nudged my shoulder with her nose.

"Only a few more minutes," I said, rubbing her face. Just then boots sounded on the road. "There they are, girl." I grabbed Krasa's rope and led her out.

Lysa was there to greet us, but it was Dolik Kitai holding on to her rope, not Uncle Roman. Dolik didn't look me in the eye, but instead stared down at my feet. My bare and dirty feet. He wore sturdy leather boots.

"Why do you have my uncle's cow?" The words came out more sharply than I intended.

"She was wandering down the road," he said, kicking a bit of dirt with the toe of his boot. "It was a good thing I was delivering medicine for Mami down this way, or Lysa may have been stolen."

I took Lysa's rope and thanked him. Then, with one rope in each hand, I turned and led the two cows toward Uncle Roman's pasture.

"Where is your uncle?" asked Dolik.

"I don't know," I said. It wasn't unusual for Uncle Roman to lose track of time, but to lose track of *Lysa?* Never. "That's why I'm going to see if I can find him."

Dolik caught up with me and took Lysa's rope back. "Let me help you."

"Aren't you worried you'll get your fancy boots dirty?"

"Why do you have to be so mean, Krystia?" he said. "I'm trying to *help* you."

"*I'm* being mean?"

Two bright red spots formed on Dolik's cheeks. "It's not *my* fault that my parents have more money than your mother. Stop holding it against me."

Was I jealous of Dolik? I had to admit that I was. But it had nothing to do with his boots or his nice clothing. Every time I saw him with his father, my heart ached. How I wished I could have one more hug from my own father. Tato's death had blasted a hole through my heart.

I opened my mouth to say something back, but no words came. Worse than that, I could feel tears welling up in my eyes. I brushed my hand across my face and continued walking in silence.

Dolik stomped along a meter behind me as we led the cows down the road toward my uncle's pasture. Strangely, even though Dolik unsettled me, I was grateful for his company. I was getting more worried about what had happened to my uncle.

We tied both cows to a tree to keep them from wandering, then split up so we could check the entire area, calling out Uncle's name as we went.

The place he most often sat was on a rock at the edge of the pasture. I liked sitting there too, because of the view of the roads and farms. I climbed up onto the rock, shouting Uncle's name, but he didn't answer. I turned, looking in all directions. No Uncle Roman. In the distance, I noticed the distinctive blue tile on the roof of Auntie Polina Semko's farmhouse. She was really an elderly distant cousin, but my sister and I called her Auntie. I had been at that farm when I was little, for a wedding. Most of the land had been taken over by a Soviet commune, but that blue roof never changed.

Dolik met back up with me, his brow creased. "Let's switch sides and try again."

About fifteen minutes later he shouted. I spotted him on the rock where I had stood, waving Uncle Roman's yellow handkerchief like a flag.

I ran over to him.

Uncle Roman lay curled on his side, deep in the brambles behind the rock. I pushed through, ignoring the thorns as they cut into me. The back of his shirt was a wet slick of blood.

Sometimes a shock is so bad that it seems you're watching your own actions from above. That's how it was for me. I lay my head on Uncle's back and begged him to get up.

"I think he's dead, Krystia," said Dolik, placing a palm on Uncle's neck. "Feel how cool he is."

I didn't want to believe it, and clung to Uncle Roman's body, begging him to wake up.

Dolik wrapped his arms around me and gently pried me away. "Take a deep breath."

I forced myself to *think*. An image crowded my thoughts. "It was the soldiers."

"What soldiers?"

"Half a dozen Soviets passed this way," I said. "And I *heard* shots, but I thought they were shooting into the air. Why would they shoot an old man looking after his cow?"

"Listen. We need to get the cows home safely," said Dolik. "But we also need to get your uncle's body out of here."

Dolik was right. But I couldn't think it all through.

"Can you stay here with him?" asked Dolik. "I'll get help."

"Go," I said.

17

Dolik nodded and left.

Even with Uncle Roman lying dead in front of me, I found it hard to believe that he was truly gone. Poor Borys and Josip and Auntie Iryna—their hearts would be broken. The pain of my own father's death was still as deep as if it had just happened. And now my cousins and auntie had their own horrible loss. My entire being ached with sorrow.

I looked down at my good skirt and shirt—both now covered with the red of blood and raspberries. I fell to my knees, hugged Uncle Roman, and wept.

CHAPTER FOUR
A VAT OF SOUP

July 1, 1941

The day after Uncle Roman's funeral, I went out to take Krasa to the pasture as usual, but a crowd of people stood in front of our church, hugging one another, laughing, and crying. Our neighbor Valentina Zhuk was in the crowd. She noticed me, ran across the road, and wrapped me in her arms. "It's happened," she said. "Ukraine is free!"

"So the Soviets are truly *gone?*"

"They are!" she said. "Look at the poster on the church door. It's a proclamation of statehood for Ukraine, independent of Germany and the Soviet Union."

I ran back into the house to wake Mama and Maria and tell them the good news. We hugged one another and twirled around the bedroom.

"Let us go tell Auntie Iryna," said Mama. "This news might cheer her a little."

Auntie was sitting at her kitchen table, her eyes brimming with tears. "How I wish my dear Roman were still alive to witness this. And that Borys and Josip were here!" She looked up. "I heard all about it on Anya's hidden wireless. The Ukrainians are broadcasting from the Lviv station. We have our independence!"

By midmorning, the poster had disappeared and huge German tanks rumbled in from the west. The slave camps, executions, hunger—these were over now. For the first time in my life, I was free. I was so excited that I threw flowers in the street. Some of the women made braided rounds of bread to welcome the German Commandant.

I stood in front of our house with Mama and Maria and watched the parade as it passed down St. Olha Street. Across the road, Nathan cheered, while Mr. and Mrs. Segal snapped pictures, just the way they always did. These Germans seemed so scrubbed and orderly compared to the ragtag Soviets. These soldiers brought us coffee and chocolate—far different from the two years of hunger, murder, and terror the Soviets had brought us. We were giddy with relief.

They made a big vat of soup in front of our church and invited all of us young people to have some. The lineup snaked down beyond the water pump at the end of our street.

Maria headed for the back of the line because Nathan was waving to her from there. I followed a few steps behind, but Dolik called out from higher up in the line, "Krystia, you can get in here."

I still felt a bit awkward around Dolik, but since Uncle Roman's death, I had begun to revise my opinion of him. He wasn't really all that unfriendly and he could be interesting to talk to. I stepped in front of him and Leon, crowded in friendly silence and moving ahead bit by bit.

One soldier stirred the huge pot of soup with a long wooden spoon, and another stood beside him, pouring one ladleful at a time into the outstretched bowls. The Commandant stood off to one side, the metallic *SS* on his collar glittering as it caught the sun.

Father Andrij stepped out of his house. This was the first time I had seen him since he'd gone into hiding from the Soviets. He walked up to the Commandant and the two men seemed to get into an intense discussion. The Commandant smiled.

Father Andrij nodded to him and pried off the planks of wood that had blocked worshippers from the church during the Soviet occupation. He turned to the crowd and cried, "Commandant Hermann says the church is now open!"

A ripple of excited cheers erupted.

The soldiers continued to ladle out soup, and before I knew it, it was my turn.

When we got back to our side of the street, Mama called, "Dolik, Leon, come in and eat with us. Your parents are already inside."

The room was crowded. Mr. and Mrs. Segal were deep in conversation with Mr. Kitai and Doctor Mina. Auntie Iryna was setting out spoons on the table. Her eyes were pink, and she was very quiet. The excitement of our new freedom was tempered by her loss and not knowing where Borys and Josip were.

And that's when I noticed Uncle Ivan. I hadn't seen him since the Soviets had set fire to his printing shop. He towered over Doctor Mina, and his clothing looked rough compared to the beautiful blue shawl she had draped over her shoulders.

I set my bowl on the table, then went over to him.

"*There's* my favorite oldest niece," he said, giving me a bear hug.

"I missed you so much, Uncle. I'm glad you're safe."

He released me but held me at arm's length. "Your mother tells me what a good help you and Maria are. I'm glad for that. Now, let us sit down to this good soup and the company of friends and family."

Mr. Kitai had set chairs from his own house around our small table. He looked up at me and grinned, the glass from his black-rimmed spectacles catching a glint of sunlight from the window. I smiled back at him. If my own father were still alive, would he look like Mr. Kitai? They would have been about the same age.

Just then Maria came in, balancing her bowl of soup. Nathan followed a few steps behind. As I looked around our crowded table, I felt almost happy. This was a true celebration.

"Let us thank God for this food," said Uncle Ivan. "And let us thank God for our many friendships."

We ate together in happy silence, savoring each spoonful. This was the most food I had eaten in a very long time.

Uncle Ivan leaned back in his chair and turned to Mr. Kitai. "Herschel," he said, "thank you for providing the paper and ink for our posters."

"My pleasure," said Mr. Kitai. "Let me know when you need more."

It took me a moment, but then I understood. "Uncle," I said, "was it *you* who printed the posters about Ukrainian independence?"

Uncle Ivan grinned.

"So your printing press is *not* destroyed?"

"Not at all. Just well hidden."

"That is wonderful," I said. "But are we truly independent? The poster disappeared and the Germans seem to be in charge."

"The Ukrainians got to Lviv right after the Soviets fled and before the Germans arrived," said Uncle Ivan. "They seized the radio station and posted signs all over, declaring Ukrainian independence. They still have control of the Lviv radio transmitter."

"So *are* we free?" I asked.

"Well . . ." said Uncle Ivan. "It's a ploy. The proclamation was a complete surprise to the Germans, but I don't think they'll be too quick to say anything, because right now the crowds see the Germans as our liberators. We're hoping the Germans will realize it's in their interest to support Ukrainian independence."

"And you know the saying," said Mr. Kitai. "Good things come from the West, bad things come from the East."

I listened in silence as the conversation continued. I hoped Uncle Ivan was right, but I couldn't help but feel queasy. These Germans did seem friendlier than the Soviets, and they had given us food and opened up the church. But for all their cleanliness and friendliness, they were still invaders.

And their flag was bloodred, just like the flag of the Soviets. I hoped that things *would* change for the better. After all, how could the Germans possibly be worse?

CHAPTER FIVE
PHOTOGRAPH

Over the next few days, the Germans settled into the buildings and houses that had been abandoned by the Soviets just days earlier. Floods of German-speaking refugees came into town on the heels of the army. These people did not speak our languages, and they didn't know our town or our customs, yet they were given jobs and were assigned the houses of people the Soviets had previously deported or executed.

Each day was filled with necessary chores. Mama still cleaned at Doctor Mina's and picked up other odd jobs as she could.

Once, as I was bringing home a pail of water, a uniformed woman with her brown hair pulled back into a tight bun stood waiting at our door.

"May I help you?" I asked, setting the pail down.

"Is this where Kataryna Fediuk lives?"

"That's my mother," I said. Had she done something to annoy the Germans? My heart pounded so hard I thought it would explode. "She hasn't done anything wrong."

The woman's forehead creased. "She's not in trouble. I just need to ask her something."

I exhaled. "This is where we live, yes, but my mother isn't home. She works as a cleaner."

"I have the right place, then," the woman said. "Didn't she clean the Tarnowsky house before the Soviet occupation?"

"She did," I said, surprised that this German would know that. It was a job Mama had taken soon after Tato died in 1936, to help make ends meet. But then the entire Tarnowsky family had been executed by the Soviets because they were rich.

"The Commandant will be living there now," said the woman. "He asked me to locate some of the old staff. Tell your mother she will start tomorrow." The woman didn't even wait for a reply before she turned and left.

When Mama got home and I told her about her new job, she sank down heavily in a kitchen chair. "That is a big place and a lot of work, but a job is a job."

Meanwhile, the radio continued to broadcast news of Ukrainian independence for three days. But then the announcements suddenly stopped.

I worried about my cousins Borys and Josip. I also hadn't seen Uncle Ivan, except for the day the Germans arrived. Why hadn't they and the other Ukrainians come out of hiding? It also worried me that the Ukrainian independence poster had disappeared so quickly. Every hour stretched out with me holding my breath, waiting to hear about whether my uncle and cousins were safe.

These new Germans were definitely settling in and making Viteretz their own. As I went about my daily chores, I noticed that each day more empty houses were filling up with either soldiers or newly arrived German families. And with so many Germans around, we were all getting more practice in speaking the language.

These new invaders were cleaner and more orderly than the Soviets, but they both had some things in common. Just like the Soviets, the Germans seemed keen on creating lists, but where the Soviets' lists were about money and education, the Germans' were about heritage. They even had researchers go through the birth records, all the way back to grandparents. They seemed most interested in German and Jewish heritage. I wondered what the Germans were up to with these lists.

To take my mind off it all, I plunged into my work, like taking Krasa to pasture, milking her, and selling whatever was left to our neighbors, either as milk, butter, or cream.

One morning when I tapped on the Segals' door to let them know their milk and butter were on the step, the door opened. "Krystia," said Mrs. Segal. "I've been meaning to show you something."

"I can't stay," I said, pushing my handcart into a shady area beside her house. "There are more deliveries to be made."

"It will only take a moment," she said, beckoning me in.

The layout of her house was similar to ours, but they had three back rooms to our one, and instead of a cowshed, they had a modern outhouse. The floor of their main room had an intricately patterned wool carpet that felt nice on the soles of my feet. Mrs. Segal's cane leaned up against the wall—she'd had polio when she was younger—but instead of using the cane, she steadied her balance by holding on to furniture. "Come to the darkroom."

My nose wrinkled at the sweet tang of the film-developing chemicals and I blinked a few times to get used to the darkness. Curved papers hung on what looked like a miniature clothesline.

"They're dry now," Mrs. Segal said, unclipping one and handing it to me.

It was a picture of Mama, with me and my sister. It had been taken as the Germans paraded down our street. Mrs. Segal's camera had caught me as I'd launched a flower into the air.

"What a wonderful photograph," I said, and I really meant it. But why did looking at it make me feel so sad? I handed it back to her.

She smiled. "It's for *you*, Krystia."

"Thank you," I said. "I will cherish this."

Dolik was standing by my handcart when I stepped back outside.

"There you are," he said. "I noticed your cart sitting here and wondered what had happened to you."

"Mrs. Segal gave me a photograph," I said, showing it to him.

He looked at it carefully. "Very nice. Your whole family together. I like how she captured the flower in midair."

His comment about my whole family—*now* I knew what bothered me about the picture. It reminded me yet again that my father was gone. A familiar sadness washed over me, but I took a deep breath and willed it away. What good would it do to always feel sorry for myself? It wouldn't bring Tato back.

I took the photo from Dolik and tucked it into my pocket. "Aren't you supposed to be delivering medicines for your mother?" I asked him.

"She doesn't have them ready yet, so I thought I'd walk with you."

It was such a sweet thing to do that I couldn't help but

smile. Why had I ever thought Dolik was unfriendly? It wasn't his fault that my father was dead.

We walked to the rest of the houses and delivered the milk, butter, and cream. Along the way we chatted.

"What's going on with your cousins?" Dolik asked. "I never see them around lately."

"I wish I knew."

"Hopefully you'll hear something soon. It must be hard on your aunt not knowing where her sons are, especially when her husband has just been buried."

"You're right. I should go over and help Auntie Iryna more. I'm sure she could use the company."

After my last delivery, Dolik went back to his house to see if his mother had the medicines ready. Instead of going immediately home, I visited Auntie Iryna for a bit, then stopped by the Fediuk Brothers' Blacksmith Shop, which had been run by Tato and Uncle Roman. The shop was on the same side of the street as our house, halfway between us and Auntie Iryna. I pushed open the door and was enveloped in cool darkness and the distinctive scent of beeswax and linseed oil.

All at once, my mind filled with an image of my father poised at his work stool, his face illuminated by coal fire. I used to sit quietly in the corner of this shop, watching as he worked the bellows to heat the forge. The back of his neck would glisten with sweat. It was like magic, seeing him transform a piece of iron into a horseshoe or hammer. Once each item was completed, he'd coat it with a mixture of beeswax and linseed oil to keep it from rusting.

As my eyes adjusted, I saw that Uncle Roman had been in the midst of making a tiny hacksaw. I picked it up and set it on the palm of my hand. The handle was finished and sealed, and the blade was cut, but the pieces hadn't been bolted together.

On a nearby shelf were nearly a dozen tiny hacksaws lined up neatly, coated in oil and wax. Why had Uncle Roman left them out in the open? Surely the Soviets had known what they were for. Many people had one of these tucked into a cuff of a sleeve or the brim of a hat. That way, if the NKVD arrested you and threw you in a boxcar, you could try to cut your way out by sawing through the hinges of a door or a barred window. With the Soviets gone, would these be needed anymore? But Uncle Roman had made them—they were likely the last things he'd made before he died. I bolted together the one he was working on, rubbed it with a cloth that smelled of oil and wax, and lined it up with the others on the shelf.

When I got home, the house was empty, so I propped the photograph from Mrs. Segal against a vase of flowers on the table. From the bedroom I got Mr. Segal's portrait of my parents' wedding and set it beside the new photograph. Now my whole family was together again, if only in pictures.

That older photograph showed Tato and Mama standing side by side in their finery, him towering over her in his dark wool suit and her looking up at him with love. Her fitted white wedding dress went down to her calves and she held a bouquet of calla lilies. There was so much promise, so much love and hope on both of their faces. What did they think their future would hold?

In the newer picture Mama had a smile on her lips, but her eyes were sad. And what would Tato think of his daughters, with their threadbare skirts and calloused hands? Had he lived, Mama's eyes would still sparkle. I missed the feel of Tato's bristly cheek when he kissed me as he tucked me in at bedtime. I missed his familiar scent of linseed oil and beeswax.

I held the wedding photo to my lips and kissed the image of Tato, and then that long-ago carefree Mama. How I wished there were something I could do to bring that hope back to her eyes.

I took a deep breath and looked at the picture of Tato one more time. He was dead, that was true, but parts of him lived on in me. He wasn't here to take the worry off Mama's face, but I was. Maria was a big help to Mama too, always stepping in to take on the tedious tasks that could wear Mama down. But Maria was afraid of every little thing, and I was the oldest. I had never really thought of it before, but now I knew. "No matter what the future has in store for us," I whispered, "I will be brave for Mama. That is my promise to you, dear Tato."

CHAPTER SIX
A WAGON

I swirled a wooden spoon through Auntie Iryna's simmering pot of blackberries and tried to judge how much longer they needed to cook before the mixture would be thick enough. On the back burner, a full kettle of water was warming up for the laundry. I didn't want to appear impatient, but it was all taking longer than I'd expected, and there wasn't much bravery in making jam.

"The fire needs to be hotter than that," said Auntie Iryna, coming in from the back room. She wrapped her apron around her fingers, gingerly opened the side door of the stove to prod the wood with an iron rod, then took the spoon from my hand, breathing in the vapors: "That smells so good," she said.

A banging at the door made us both jump. Dolik stood there, out of breath and eyes wide.

"What's happened?" Auntie Iryna asked.

"Mami got a phone call from a friend in Velicky Selo," he said. "They've found corpses in the prison."

Auntie Iryna's body swayed. "Josip . . . Borys . . . Please God, tell me it isn't them."

"Mami says they're bringing the bodies out and they need to be identified."

"I have to get there," said Auntie Iryna. She was so unsteady on her feet that I was afraid she would fall.

Velicky Selo was on the way to Lviv, about ten kilometers from Viteretz. Auntie could not walk there on her own in her current state. "I'll go with you," I said.

But she'd put a kerchief over her hair and was out the door and marching down the street before she finished tying the knot under her chin.

Dolik ran after her. "I'll find a wagon."

At first I wondered why Dolik was looking for a wagon, but all at once I winced. If my cousins were dead, we'd need to bring their bodies back for burial.

I watched him rushing down the street, looking for someone with a wagon to borrow. I was grateful for Dolik being so helpful—he'd been the same when Uncle Roman was killed—but I felt a surge of jealousy too. How I wished I were him, with both a mother *and* father, plenty of food to eat, and even a telephone. Dolik didn't have a care in the world.

But even as those thoughts crowded my mind, they shamed me. Dolik was trying to help, and Auntie Iryna was on her way to Velicky Selo without me. And what was *I* doing? Moping around, feeling sorry for myself. So much for being brave!

I dashed back into the house, set the steaming pot of berries onto the kitchen table and covered it with a cloth, then closed up the vents on the stove to starve the fire.

As I ran out the door, I nearly plowed into Maria, who was lugging a pail of water for the garden.

"You look like you've seen a ghost, Krystia," she said.

I told her about the corpses at Velicky Selo and her eyes filled with tears. "I should go with Auntie," she said. "It's not fair that you have to do the hard things all the time."

"But you carry all those buckets of water every day *and* hoe and weed two gardens," I said. "We each have our strengths, Maria. I'll go with Auntie."

She hugged me, then held me at arm's length to look me in the eye. "One day I hope to be as brave as you."

I brushed away a piece of hair that had fallen in front of her face. "One day, Sister, I hope to be as strong as *you*."

Maria smiled at that. "Hurry," she said. "Look how far Auntie has already gone without you."

I started down the street, then turned back. "When you're done your chores, could you go help Mama at the Commandant's? She was expecting me."

"I'll try," called Maria.

I caught up with Auntie Iryna—Dolik was nowhere to be seen—and together we walked in grim silence. We were a kilometer out of town when the sound of truck tires crunched on the road behind us. The driver was the same soldier who had ladled out soup to us. He opened the window and stuck out his head.

"A boy told me that you're going to Velicky Selo."

Auntie Iryna looked at him blankly and nodded.

"I need to be there as well," he said. "So why don't I take you? There's not enough room in the front for three, but you can ride in the back."

The offer surprised me. Dolik must not have been able to track down the dogcatcher or Mr. Bilinski, the two people in our neighborhood with wagons. I didn't relish getting into a truck with a soldier, and I was certain that Auntie felt the same, but we didn't have the time to be choosy.

"Thank you," said Auntie Iryna.

I scrambled in first, then held Auntie's hand as she climbed up.

We gripped on to the truck's side as the soldier sped toward Velicky Selo, careening left and right to avoid potholes. In less than half an hour the truck reached the main square of town. Dozens of women crowded in front of the municipal building where the prison was housed.

My nose crinkled at the sickly whiff of decay. Lumpy gray tarps were lined up on the grass not far from the women.

"When the Soviets fled, they left these corpses to rot in the basement of that building," said the soldier as he undid the tailgate and motioned for us to get out. "The locals have been viewing the bodies, but there are quite a few that they can't identify, so they're not from Velicky Selo. We've got to clear them out or there will be an outbreak of disease."

Auntie slid out of the truck bed and strode down the street. I followed her, my feet feeling like lead.

She knelt beside the first mound and pulled back the tarp, revealing the mottled face of a young stranger, his hair darkened and stiff with blood. She crawled to the next body and I did the same.

The odor of decay wafted up and I held my breath. I stood a meter or so from where Auntie knelt. I wished I could have helped her more with this awful job, but it took all my willpower not to break down and weep. Why had the Soviets killed these men?

I helped Auntie back to her feet after she had pulled the cloth over the last corpse in the line.

Just then Commandant Hermann stepped out through the double doors of the building. Pairs of soldiers came out behind him, carrying more bodies covered with tarps. These were lined up beside the ones we had just checked. A stronger wave of stench wafted over to us.

As Auntie Iryna and the other women rushed to the new row of corpses, I was nearly knocked to the ground. A wail rose up and a woman cried, "My son!"

One by one, many of the dead were claimed. And as the crowd thinned, I found Auntie on her knees, cradling a corpse so mutilated that the face was unrecognizable. I knelt down beside her.

"Josip, dear Josip," she murmured.

I was about to ask her how she knew, but then I noticed his crooked baby finger.

The shock of recognition was like a punch in the gut. If it hadn't been for his crooked baby finger, Josip's body could have been left unclaimed. I took a few gasping breaths to calm myself, then got up and left Auntie Iryna so she could grieve her son. There were still more bodies to look at, and one more family member I dreaded finding, but it had to be done.

Auntie Iryna and I were the last to leave. We did not find Borys and I was grateful for that. The soldier who had driven helped us load Josip into his truck, and we made the sad journey home.

When we arrived at Auntie's house, I was enveloped in the steamy scent of cooked blackberries. The pot was still cooling on the kitchen table, the preserve jars all lined up, ready to be filled. It seemed a lifetime ago that we had been busy with the mundane chore of making jam. Had that really just been this morning? I lifted the pot off the table and set it back onto the stove, then cleared away the jars. The soldier laid Josip's broken body onto the table and walked out the door.

Auntie Iryna wrapped her arms around her son and wept.

I stood there helplessly, wishing that there was something I could do to help. The lingering aroma of blackberries comforted me, to think that Josip's body was now wrapped in the scent of home, rather than the stench of that prison.

I took the cloth off the pot and dipped in a wooden spoon. The jam had thickened while we were gone. I lined up the jars again and filled them one by one.

"Go, Krystia," said Auntie Iryna once I had finished. "Get your mother. She and I will prepare Josip's body together."

I ran to the Tarnowsky house, the largest residence in our main square. I felt out of place as I stood in front of it, barefoot and smelling of death. I rapped loudly on the door. It cracked open and Mama stared out at me. She pulled me quickly inside. "Krystia, come in, but from now on, use the servants' entrance at the back."

The place seemed huge on the inside. Before it had been ravaged by the Soviets, it must have looked elegant as well. A gilded chain hung from the ceiling overhead—it had probably held a chandelier. The central hallway opened up to a curved wooden staircase that looked as if it had once been covered in carpet that had been pulled off, leaving rows of bent nails and scratched wood. Pale rectangular patches covered the walls. One was the size of that old painting of Princess Tarnowska, the portrait that had been carted away by the Bronseks. The whole place had a musty, rotting smell, and bits of wood and broken china were scattered all over the floor.

Mama leaned toward me and sniffed, then covered her mouth with one hand. "Maria told me where you were going. I'm almost afraid to ask if you were able to identify any bodies."

"We found Josip."

She gasped and hugged me and we both wept. She took a deep shuddering breath, then said, "You didn't find Borys?"

"No, thank God. We can only hope that he's still alive."

"I'll go to Iryna right away," said Mama, untying her apron and handing it to me. She looked around at the house with panic in her eyes.

"Don't worry. I'll stay here with Maria," I said. "We'll continue to clean."

CHAPTER SEVEN
REFUGE

It is a terrible thing, to break the earth still fresh from death and to bury a son beside his father. I don't know how Auntie Iryna gathered the strength to greet all the people who came out for the evening *Panikheda* at the church. Auntie Polina had made the trek from her blue-roofed house in the country.

After the simple wooden casket was carried outside the next morning and we stood at Josip's open grave, I scanned the faces of people crowded round. Through a haze of tears, I thought I saw Borys, but when I blinked, he was gone.

Auntie Iryna received a steady stream of visitors to her house after the funeral. Mama, Maria, and I stayed to lend our support, but also to make sure Auntie didn't wear herself out. Had she even slept since Josip's body was found? And her mind must be filled with worry about Borys.

Auntie Polina lingered for an hour after the last person left, sitting with Auntie Iryna and reminiscing about happier times. "When we were children, we had a cow race," she said. "Do you remember that?"

Auntie Iryna tried to smile. "How could I forget?"

Auntie Polina looked from me to Maria and said, "I got up on the back of our black cow, and your aunt rode our neighbors' dappled cow."

"I can't imagine cows running," said Maria.

"They didn't," said Auntie Polina, grinning.

Auntie Iryna's smile became wider. "We sat on those stupid cows for about fifteen minutes."

"Do you remember the bonfire?" asked Auntie Polina.

Auntie Iryna leaned back into her chair with her eyes closed. "That's when I met Roman. I'll never forget the bonfire."

It was good to see Auntie Iryna's sadness lifted for a short while by the happy memories. When Auntie Polina got up to leave, I followed her out the door. "Let me know if I can help in any way," she said, giving me a hug.

Mama made Auntie Iryna a cup of linden tea, and we were about to leave when a shadow filled the door.

It was Commandant Hermann.

Auntie Iryna stumbled to her feet to greet him.

"I am sorry for your loss," he said, but his face didn't look as if he meant it, and his eyes didn't focus on my aunt's face. Instead, his gaze assessed her house. "Your blacksmith shop is now vacant; this house is too big for one person. You cannot stay here," he said. "A German family will have this house."

Auntie's lower lip trembled. "But where will I go?"

"Your family can take you in," he said, glancing from Mama to me and Maria.

"I have just buried my husband, and now my son, and you are forcing me to leave my house?"

"You were scheduled for removal this morning," said the Commandant. "It was in sympathy for your loss that we waited for the funeral to be over. Now, good day. Pack up your clothing and some food, but everything else is to remain in the house."

With that, he was gone.

"That man is vile," I said. "And of all days to throw you out."

"What will become of me now?" said Auntie Iryna, collapsing back into her chair. She cradled her head on the table and wept.

"We're happy to have you," said Mama. But what she didn't say was that it would be difficult to feed all of us, especially come winter. The loss of Auntie's house also meant losing her vegetable garden and patch of wheat, yet we would be gaining a mouth to feed. But one advantage of being poor is that it doesn't take long to pack. We bundled Auntie's meager selection of clothing around jars of preserves.

"What the Commandant doesn't know won't hurt him," said Mama, hastily opening and closing drawers and removing everything she could find. She packed up Auntie's linens and cutlery and plates. "We'll store these extra things in Krasa's loft, beside the items from Auntie Stefa. Now, what about your cow and chickens?"

"I assumed Lysa and the chickens would come with *me*." Auntie Iryna paused from her packing. "He didn't specifically say to *leave* the cow and chickens."

"The cow and chickens are not in the house," I added. "He told you to leave everything *in the house*."

"But if the Commandant finds two cows in our shed, then what?" asked Maria. "He'll think we've stolen one of them."

This conversation was making me very angry. "All I know is that right now Lysa needs to go to the pasture," I said. "And so does Krasa. You can tell me what you decide about the cow when I get back."

"You're right, Krystia," said Auntie Iryna. "Take the cows to the pasture."

Maria pulled our milk cart piled with Auntie's meager belongings, and I walked close behind her, leading Lysa. Mama and Auntie Iryna walked a few steps in front of us, each cradling a canvas bag with a trembling chicken inside.

As we passed our blacksmith shop, I remembered what Uncle Roman had been working on before he was killed. "Maria," I said, "hold Lysa's rope. There's something I need to get." I took a towel from the cart and filled it with the small hacksaws.

Once we got to our house, I untethered Krasa and made the sad journey to our pasture with both cows. The incoming traffic was so heavy it was hard to keep the cows out of the way. Mostly the traffic was wide military trucks, but there were also ragged refugees pushing wheelbarrows loaded with their belongings—and others coming with nothing.

I watched an exhausted woman and a girl my age as they approached. The mother leaned heavily on a wooden staff and her shoes were held together with rags. On the girl's back was a small knapsack. When we were nearly face-to-face, I greeted them both with a smile. "Good day," I said in German.

The woman surprised me by answering in Ukrainian, "Good day." Then she asked, "Could you spare some milk for my daughter?"

"You need it more than I do, Mutter," said the girl, wrapping her arm around her mother's waist.

Who were these people? The other soldiers and the civilians who had recently come to Viteretz didn't understand Ukrainian at all.

"I can spare some milk for both of you," I said. "Follow me."

I led the cows down a quiet laneway. The mother sat on a pile of rubble, stretching her feet out in front of her. The daughter knelt on the ground beside her.

Krasa nudged the daughter's cheek. The girl patted Krasa's nose. "We had a beautiful spotted cow like yours back home," the girl said.

"Where was home?"

"Bukovyna," said the girl.

"So you're Ukrainian?"

"We're German," said the mother.

"Germans, but from the *South*?" I asked. It didn't make sense.

"Most people in Bukovyna are Slavs," said the mother. "Like you, Ukrainian. Or Romanian. But there were German communities in Bukovyna too."

"The Soviets put my father in a slave-labor camp in Siberia," said the girl. "Mutter and I were rescued by the Germans. This whole area is now part of the Reich, so there will be a lot more of us Volksdeutsche settling here."

"Volksdeutsche?"

"Ethnic Germans from the Slavic countries," the mother explained.

This conversation made me think of the lists the Germans made, and how they thought Germans were better. But even though people from Viteretz were suffering because of the German occupation, this bedraggled mother and daughter hadn't had it easy either. They were stuck in the middle of warring countries just like we were.

"Let me get you that milk," I said.

The girl took a battered tin cup from her knapsack and handed it to me.

I rubbed my face against Krasa's cheek and whispered, "I know it's not time to milk you, but just a cup?"

Krasa snorted as if she understood. I knelt down and milked her, then handed the cup to the mother. I felt sorry for them, but where would all these Volksdeutsche live? Where would *we* all live?

"Thank you for your kindness," said the mother. "And at least tell me your name."

"I'm Krystia Fediuk."

"Good to meet you, Krystia Fediuk. My name is Frau Gertrude Schneider, and this is Marga, my daughter."

"Good luck to both of you," I said as I grabbed the cows' tethers and started back on my way to the pasture.

"Get your fill," I said to Lysa as I let her off the rope so she could graze in Auntie Iryna's pasture. "Who knows what will happen to you tomorrow?"

As the cows grazed, I sat on Uncle Roman's rock and watched the road. So many Germans coming to our town—including ragged Volksdeutsche fleeing the Soviet Union, better-off civilians coming from Germany, and the military.

Standing on top of the rock, I could see the surrounding countryside where Ukrainian farmers had lived for hundreds of years. It made me wonder whether the whole area would soon be filled with Germans.

I spotted the familiar blue-roofed house and wondered if Polina Semko was home yet. And that gave me an idea. Auntie Polina could take Lysa for now. That way, we wouldn't raise suspicions by having two cows in our shed, yet Auntie Iryna wouldn't have to give up Lysa.

"Sorry to do this to you, Krasa," I said, caressing the cow's neck one last time as I left her tethered in a hidden shady spot in Auntie Iryna's pasture. "I'll be back as soon as I can."

I wrapped Lysa's rope around my fist and led her off the main road and through a grassy shortcut. The walk took nearly an hour, and many of the farms I passed had already been taken over by new people. As I led Lysa onward, I had a growing sense that the Germans had not come to liberate Ukraine, but to take us over.

The familiar blue roof came into view. Thankfully, there was no truck around, or soldiers, but Polina Semko's buildings and fields were in shambles. Just a portion of her house still stood, and her barn looked like a lean-to. The fruit trees had been hacked down, and where wheat should have been growing, there were only weeds.

I rapped on her door. "Auntie Polina, are you home?"

She stepped out and looked from me to Lysa. "Krystia! What are you doing here?"

"Any chance you'd be able to look after Auntie Iryna's cow?" I explained about Auntie Iryna being forced out of her house.

"I can keep her here," said Auntie Polina. "And I'll appreciate the milk, as my only cow is dry."

"What happened to your farm, Auntie?"

She threw up her hands in frustration. "The Soviets, of course."

"Do you have enough to live on?"

Her eyes sparkled. "I have a cow that gives milk now. And the Soviets couldn't steal or destroy *everything*. I will get by as I always have."

By the time I got back to the pasture, Krasa had worked herself free of her tether, but fortunately she hadn't wandered off. She was happily munching away at a patch of grass under some trees. I wrapped her rope around my fist and gave it a gentle tug. "Come on, Krasa," I said. "Mama will wonder what is taking us so long."

Ahead of me on the road were soldiers who were gathering the newly arriving refugees into a work unit. One of them was passing out shovels, and a second was giving instructions. I overheard snippets of conversation—something about digging a ditch in the woods.

I stayed a dozen or so meters behind the group practically all the way home and watched as it grew in size. I felt sorry for these refugees. Even before they could rest for the night or find something to eat, they were being assigned to heavy labor. I didn't see Frau Schneider or her daughter in the group, but they would have been farther ahead, as it had taken me some time to get Lysa into the country. Had they been assigned work as well?

When I finally got home, Mama was standing on our doorstep, hands on her hips and a worried look on her face.

She followed me to the shed as I settled Krasa in. "Where is Lysa?" she asked.

"With Auntie Polina," I said.

Mama's face lit up. "Good thinking."

In the wee hours of the night, low voices in the kitchen startled me awake. One was Auntie's, and another . . . Could it be? I crept silently out of bed, taking care not to wake Mama or Maria. I had to see for myself. With Auntie Iryna was Cousin Borys!

"You're alive," I whispered, running to him and wrapping my arms around his neck, breathing in the scent of smoke and pine as I hugged him tight. "I was so worried about you!"

"I'm not ready to die yet, my dear cousin," he said, planting a kiss on the top of my head.

"I thought I saw you at Josip's funeral."

"I was there briefly," he said. "But I didn't want the Germans to see me. And I cannot stay long now. Go back to bed, Krystia, and don't wake your mother or sister. I came to see Mama so we could remember Josip together. And I'm trying to convince her to come with me to the forest."

"Will you visit again?" I asked.

"There are things that need to be done," he said. "But I'm never far away."

"Stay safe, Borys," I said, hugging him again before reluctantly going back to the bedroom.

As I tried to get to sleep, I thought about what Borys had said about things that needed to be done, and that maybe Auntie Iryna would be going to the forest to live with him. What were they working on?

CHAPTER EIGHT
AN ACT OF TREASON

When I got back from the pasture the next morning, people were clustered around the closed doors of our church. I stood on my toes to peer over their shoulders and saw Dolik close to the front. I wormed my way through the crowd and poked him. "What's so interesting?"

"A poster. All the original townspeople are ordered to assemble in the main square today at noon," he said. "Any disobedience will be considered an act of treason."

Treason meant death. My knees suddenly felt weak. "I need to find Mama."

"I saw her go to the Tarnowsky place about an hour ago. But I haven't seen her since."

As I rushed into town, I passed a large group of ragged and tired newcomers, and like the refugees from yesterday, they were carrying shovels. These ones were mostly men, and younger. From the fresh dirt smeared on their clothing and faces, it looked like they were on their way back from a job.

When I got to the Tarnowsky house, I hurried upstairs to find Mama. She was on her hands and knees, scrubbing the bathroom floor. She sat back on her heels and looked at me.

"Mama, there's an important notice," I said. "All the original inhabitants must come to the town square at noon, and those who don't will be considered traitors."

"The square's just outside," said Mama, pushing a loose piece of hair away from her eye. "I'll go out as soon as the municipal clock begins to chime."

"But what about Borys and Uncle Ivan?" I whispered.

"Neither was counted on the Germans' lists, so they won't be missed—" Suddenly, Mama stood up and ripped off her apron. "But your *sister*! I sent her to look for stray eggs in the fields. She may not even know about this order. You need to finish this room for me. If Frau Hermann comes in, introduce yourself."

She shoved the apron at me and left.

I stepped out of the servants' door just as the clock in the square rang out the first of twelve chimes. It seemed that everyone in town, both original and newcomers, had crowded in to hear what the Commandant had to say. Even in this back alleyway it was hard to move with the crush of people.

I tried to press forward, but a large man stumbled backward and his boot landed on my big toe. I screamed.

"Sorry, girl," said the man, grabbing my arm as I balanced on one foot. "You're not going to have much luck getting through here."

He was right. Everywhere I looked was a wall of people. The huge crowd gave us all some anonymity, though. Even if Mama couldn't find Maria, perhaps she wouldn't be missed.

I still needed to hear the announcement for myself, and I figured walking through the Tarnowsky house would get me closer to the front of the crowd than trying to push any farther through the alley. I hobbled back into the servants' entrance, holding on to furniture and railings as I went. I had just placed my hand on the front-door handle when the clomping of boots sounded on the floor behind me. I did a hop-turn on one foot to see who it was.

Commandant Hermann.

"You're the cleaner's daughter, aren't you?" he asked, his light brown eyebrows creasing into a frown.

"I am, Herr Commandant," I said. "I was helping my mother today."

"You should be outside with the others."

"I am sorry, Herr Commandant," I said, bowing slightly, still balancing on one foot and clutching the door handle for balance. "I was out in the alleyway but got pushed back in. And someone nearly crushed my toe. I'm going out the front door."

He glanced down at my toe and then back at my face. "You can't use the front door. Go upstairs. You can watch from the balcony."

"Yes, Herr Commandant," I said, bowing again. "Thank you, Herr Commandant."

When I got to the big bedroom, I opened the latch on the double windows and stepped out onto the balcony. I could see the entire town square and all the people heaving and pushing down below.

Maria was there, thank goodness! She and Nathan were at the opposite end of the square, their backs nearly pinned against the wall of the bakery. Mama and Auntie Iryna stood close by, in front of the New Synagogue, which shared a wall with the bakery. Above them, Petro Zhuk sat cross-legged on the flat roof of the New Synagogue. Close to Mama were Mr. Kitai and Doctor Mina, with Leon and Dolik.

It felt odd to be up here with everyone else across the square and on the ground. I wondered whether, centuries ago, old Princess Tarnowska would gaze down at her subjects from here.

Mr. Segal stood on the top step of our town hall, his camera pointed at a few soldiers who were directing the crowd to leave a wide-open space in the middle of the square. Mrs. Segal stood beside her husband, without her cane, taking pictures of civilians instead of soldiers. She turned her camera to me and clicked.

A couple of soldiers walked from the square toward me, clearing a path for the Commandant. One of them was the soldier who had helped us retrieve Josip's body. The big double doors creaked open below me as Commandant Hermann stepped out. I peered over the balcony and saw the round top of his cap, and his shoulders with their *SS* epaulettes. He marched with the soldiers to the open space in the middle of the square.

The crowd was suddenly quiet.

"If you hear your name, you must come forward," announced the Commandant.

A soldier handed him a sheet of paper.

I looked around the crowd and said a silent prayer: *Please don't call Mama's name. Please don't call Auntie Iryna's.*

"Samuel Steinburg," the Commandant said, reading from the paper.

Our dogcatcher.

There were whispers in front of the synagogue, and then the crowd parted. Samuel Steinburg stepped farther into the square, wringing his leather cap.

"Aaron Bronsky."

A skinny young man wearing a white apron over a white shirt and pants emerged from the cluster near the bakery and stood beside the dogcatcher.

"David Kohn . . . Zachary Goldblum . . ."

More names were called that I didn't recognize, but I kept count of the number. One hundred had been called, all men of army age. It seemed to me that the names could all be Jewish.

"These hundred men standing before you are murderers!" said Commandant Hermann in a loud and clear voice.

There was a collective gasp from the crowd.

"These Jews are guilty of torturing, mutilating, and killing the hundreds of men that we found in the prisons of Velicky Selo."

That was not true! The *Soviets* had done the killing. Why would the Commandant say that?

"I sentence them to death," said the Commandant, pacing.

A hum of whispers and shrieks punctured the air.

"Kill them!" shouted a man's voice from the depths of the crowd. A woman that I didn't know chimed in, "The Jews deserve to die. Let's get them all."

The Commandant stopped pacing. He looked out into the crowd, almost as if he expected more people to say awful things about Jews.

"Shut your drunken mouth!" yelled Petro Zhuk from the rooftop.

Silence.

Commandant Hermann scanned the crowd, as if trying to pinpoint where that shout had come from.

My mind was whirling. Those who had murdered our men were long gone back to Moscow. The hundred men now huddled in the square had suffered under the Soviets just as we *all* had.

The crowd was silent as Commandant Hermann paced. It was as if he were a match and we were his dry wood. But the crowd had not yet begun to burn.

Just then I noticed some movement from across the square. Mr. Kitai had left Doctor Mina and Dolik and Leon and was pushing through to the edge of the crowd. "Commandant Hermann," he said in a polite but firm voice, "those murders were an affront to us all, and we all thank you for trying to punish the culprits."

A murmur of agreement rippled through some of the onlookers.

"But *these* men did not do it."

"He's right!" a woman shouted.

"It was the Soviet secret police—the NKVD—who killed and tortured those young men, but the murderers left *before* you got here," Mr. Kitai went on. "If I may . . . Herr

61

Commandant . . . my own father fought in the German army during the Great War. You saved us from the Russians then. We thank you for ousting the Soviets now."

"And whom might you be?" asked the Commandant.

He bowed his head slightly. "Mr. Herschel Kitai at your service, Herr Commandant."

"You are Jewish?" the Commandant asked.

"I am, Herr Commandant," Mr. Kitai said in a clear and strong voice. "And like these men who have been gathered together, we admire German culture and democracy."

I felt myself nodding in agreement.

"Stand with these murderers," the Commandant ordered.

I gasped.

Mr. Kitai stayed where he was for a long, silent moment. Then he took one deep breath and said, "I will stand with the others who have been unjustly accused."

"Take them all," Commandant Hermann ordered the soldiers.

"Please," cried Dolik, pushing through the onlookers. "Don't kill my father!"

It was as if the air had been sucked out of the square. The Commandant regarded Dolik. "You can die with him if you like, boy."

Doctor Mina rushed over, wrapped her arm around Dolik's waist, and yanked him backward, into the crowd.

"You will control your brat in future, madam, if you know what is good for you," said the Commandant.

Dolik struggled to get out of his mother's grip.

The Commandant paced some more and looked out into the crush of people. Behind him, his soldiers pointed their Lugers at the hundred and one Jewish scapegoats. The men were herded off the square toward Esther Street. Mr. Kitai had his eyes fixed on his family as he was marched out.

From my vantage point, I could see where they were heading—to the wooded area beside the Jewish cemetery.

No one in the crowd spoke.

The Commandant stopped pacing. He rested a palm on the holster of his own Luger and glared at people in the crowd. "I am your Commandant," he said. "You had best remember that. We have plenty of room for new graves."

He turned and walked back toward me—and into the Tarnowsky house.

CHAPTER NINE
BLACK-FRAMED EYEGLASSES

I was frozen to my spot on the balcony. Doctor Mina gripped Dolik and the two of them stumbled together toward home, Maria, Nathan, and Auntie Iryna close behind. A few meters behind them was Mama, who held a flailing Leon in both arms.

The Commandant wouldn't really have all those men killed, would he? Was this a ploy to scare us?

The Commandant approached the house, but not once did he look up. I guess he didn't think of me at all—which was a good thing—but I desperately didn't want to be in his house when he got here. I would make my escape using the servants' stairs at the back.

I turned. And gasped.

A woman blocked the balcony door. Her light brown hair framed a hard-looking face. "What are you doing on my balcony?"

"It's an . . . an honor to meet you, Frau Hermann," I said, my heart still pounding from what I had just witnessed. "My name is Krystia Fediuk. My mother is Kataryna Fediuk. She cleans for the Commandant, and my sister and I help her." The words tumbled out breathlessly. "Commandant Hermann told me to attend the announcement from here."

"What an odd thing for him to do," said Frau Hermann. "He is a very kind man, though, so in some ways not unexpected."

His performance in the town square was not the act of a kind man. Ensuring that I would witness everything clearly was also not the act of a kind man. But I bobbed my head and said, "Yes, ma'am, he very *kindly* let me watch from here because someone stepped on my toe and I couldn't get through the crowd."

She glanced at my toe, which was now red and slightly swollen. "You can finish your cleaning now."

I had just witnessed my friend's father being marched into the woods along with a hundred other innocent men, and this woman wanted me to finish cleaning? Just looking at her made me feel ill.

"Mama and I will be back tomorrow, Frau Hermann," I said in as calm and humble a voice as I could muster. "But there are chores I need to do at home."

Her brow furrowed. "You Slavs are all alike. You can't think further than your own shallow needs."

With that, she turned and walked away from the balcony. I watched her exit into the hallway, then heard her high heels click-clacking down the curving front staircase. I followed a few steps behind, then exited by the servants' door.

As I limped down the street, I was jolted still by the deafening staccato of gunshots. Was this what the execution of a hundred and one victims sounded like?

My conscience swirled. Why had I been so selfish, praying only for *my* family? I should have prayed for Dolik's family too—for everyone in our town. I wanted to find Dolik—but I needed time to think.

I wondered if what I'd heard wasn't really an execution. Maybe it was distant thunder or the sounds of war. Would the Commandant really go through with killing a hundred and one innocent men? It just didn't seem possible.

I pushed through the noisy crowds until I got to my own street. As I passed our blacksmith shop, I saw that the door was slightly open. I was surprised to hear the familiar rhythm of metal banging on metal—almost as if my father were calling to me. I slipped through the door and the sound got louder. The scent of beeswax and linseed oil almost made me weep. The forge was lit, and a man was shaping a piece of iron into a horseshoe.

How I longed to see Tato just one more time. Tato would tell me what was going on and what I should do about it. This man in here now was like his ghost. When he raised his head and took off his mask, the spell was broken. His hair was blond, where Tato's was dark, and this man's build was much slighter.

"Greetings, Fräulein," said the man with a smile. "Don't tell me they sent *you* to be my apprentice."

My mouth opened, but no words came out. I took a deep breath and held on to the door to keep my balance.

"I won't bite," he said. "Did you just step in to get away from the crowds?"

I nodded, then found my voice. "My father was a blacksmith. This was his shop."

"The Soviets probably killed him, is that correct?" said the man.

"Cancer," I replied. "But my uncle Roman, who was a blacksmith here as well—he was killed by the Soviets."

The man set the tongs that still held a half-shaped horseshoe onto the forge and removed his work glove. He reached out his hand. "I'm Wolfgang Zimmer," he said. "And who might you be?"

"Krystia Fediuk," I said, gripping his hand in mine. "I live a few doors down."

"Drop by any time, Fräulein Krystia."

"Thank you, Herr Zimmer." I said. He seemed nice enough, but the whole situation was wrong. He had been rewarded with my family's shop just because he was German. Dolik's father may have been executed today just because he was Jewish.

I slipped back outside.

The street was nearly empty now, but I didn't want to go home and I couldn't bear to see Dolik just yet.

I made my way to the Jewish cemetery that backed onto the woods. I needed to see for myself what had really happened. If the Commandant had just been trying to scare us, I'd have good news for Dolik. But maybe the men had been beaten. Maybe they needed help.

I hid behind a weathered tombstone close to the edge of the woods. Voices drifted in the wind, but the words were mostly indistinct. I stepped closer, keeping behind a leafy bush.

"The shoes. Sort them by size." A *woman's* voice. And not a soldier. It sounded like some sort of meeting.

I stepped from behind the bush and walked toward the voices.

The Germans who weren't from Germany: Volksdeutsche refugees. A few were tossing loose soil from a mound onto what looked like a freshly turned garden. Other shovels were neatly piled to the side.

Most of the Germans were calmly sorting through mounds of clothing. Shirts here, jackets there, hats there. As a shirt was picked up and shaken out, then folded, I couldn't see a bullet hole, and there was no blood. All of the clothing seemed undamaged. But where were the Jewish men?

And then I noticed a familiar face—Frau Schneider, but her daughter, Marga, wasn't with her. Frau Schneider was picking through the clothing along with several men and one other woman. One of the soldiers who had been handing out shovels yesterday stood among them, giving orders. They all seemed so calm, just concentrating on sorting the clothing.

So these people had been sent out here first to dig what looked like a garden ready for planting, and then they were sorting clothing? Very odd. And what would they be planting in the middle of the woods?

I was staring at the huge mound of loose soil, trying to figure that out, when I noticed a barely perceptible tremor. Was it my imagination? But as I watched, the ground trembled again. A clump of dirt crumbled, revealing a flash of white. I squinted.

A hand, fingers reaching out.

All at once I realized what I was staring at. The men *had* been murdered. And this was their grave.

I had an image in my mind of what must have happened. The victims marched to the edge of the ditch and then ordered to remove their clothing. They were shot, and fell into the ditch, and dirt was shoveled over them. The tremors I'd noticed must have been caused by the bodies settling into the earth. The mass murder was horrible, but to force the men to remove their clothing first so it wouldn't be damaged?

A wave of nausea coursed through me and I bent over, clutching my stomach. I fell to the ground and the world swirled.

"Krystia, what are you doing here?"

Frau Schneider's voice.

I propped myself up and tried to focus. A tall man holding a shovel hovered above me, standing beside Frau Schneider. He prodded me with the tip of it. "You shouldn't be here," he said.

"It's all right," said Frau Schneider. "I know her."

The man tossed down the shovel and walked away.

I sucked in huge gulps of air and tried to get to my

feet, but my knees were too weak. One of Frau Schneider's hands was level with my face. She held several pairs of eyeglasses, but there was one that caught my eye. They had round black frames. Mr. Kitai's.

I looked up at Frau Schneider's placid face. Was she evil? She seemed unaffected by the job she was doing.

"Those glasses," I said. "Could I have them?"

"These old things?" She looked surprised. "They're supposed to go to the Volksdeutsche families, but here, take them."

"Thank you," I said, shoving them inside my pocket. I stumbled to my feet and limped away.

When I passed Auntie Iryna's house, or what *had* been her house, the door opened and Marga stepped out, blocking my way.

"The neighbors told me this was your aunt's house," she said.

"Yes, Marga, it was." I didn't want to talk with her right then, especially after seeing what her mother had been doing in the woods.

"You stole from us," she said. "I saw feathers out back. There should be chickens here. And our cow. I saw you with *two* cows. One of them was supposed to be *ours*."

There was so much that I wanted to say to her, but what was the point? "My friend Dolik . . . his father was just executed," I said, stepping around her. "I need to find him."

"I'm going to tell the Commandant that you stole our cow," she said. "Your whole family is going to be in big trouble."

Did she realize just how much trouble she could get us into? I stepped farther to the side to walk around her.

She stepped back in front of me and poked my chest with her finger. "This isn't the end of it."

"I'm sorry, Marga, but I really have to go," I said as I hurried away from her, past the blacksmith shop that also used to be ours. The rhythmic pounding of metal upon metal sounded through the door, and I imagined Herr Zimmer working steadily just the way Tato used to.

At the Kitais' house, I pushed on the front door and was about to step in, but I could hear Dolik arguing with his mother. I closed the door quietly and sat on the doorstep, leaning against the cool stone wall. Snippets of the argument came through the door—Dolik upset with his mother for pulling him away when he tried to get to his father. "We can't all act like sheep!" he shouted.

It was hard to hear Doctor Mina's response, because she wasn't shouting, but it was clear that Dolik was in no mood for comforting. I stood up and brushed the creases from my skirt, and as I did so, I felt the outline of Mr. Kitai's glasses in my pocket. I sat back down, cradling my head in my arms.

The door creaked open. Leon stepped out. "Krystia," he said, slumping down beside me and leaning against my shoulder, "what do you think is going to happen to Tate?"

He looked so tiny huddled beside me. I wanted to say something comforting, but all that came out was a sob. I wrapped my arm around his shoulder and together we wept.

As I got undressed for bed that night, Mr. Kitai's glasses slipped out of my skirt pocket and fell onto the floor. I picked them up and felt the weight of them in my hand. This was all that was left of a man I had known my whole life.

I set the glasses down on the table in front of the wedding picture of Mama and Tato, then climbed into bed beside Maria. How I longed for a simple life, where fathers lived to see their children grow, and where governments didn't kill. Sleep would not come, that I knew, but I closed my eyes and tried to think of nothing.

CHAPTER TEN
SEEING

It was impossible to think of nothing. When I closed my eyes, I saw that fresh grave with the trembling earth. What kind of government would allow the Commandant to kill innocent people? The *Soviets* had done this sort of thing. Clearly, these Germans were no better. It made sense now that these Germans and the Soviets had been on the same side of the war for the past two years.

Maybe we had been wrong to welcome them so readily. These were not the cultured Germans who believed in democracy and brought freedom. I thought about the lists they kept making. From what I could sort out, they believed that Aryans—a term they used to describe people like themselves—deserved extra privileges. But what else did they believe in? I was almost afraid to find out.

I thought about the words I'd overheard when the organizers talked among themselves. *They* didn't call themselves Germans. They called themselves Nazis, because of things they believed in. I sat up in bed, and as my eyes adjusted to the dimness, I looked at Maria, fast asleep but with a face etched in grief. It was too dark to see either Mama or Auntie Iryna in the big bed across the room, but I could hear their rhythmic breathing.

And then I remembered Marga's threat.

What if she told the Commandant that I'd stolen her cow? Could I be punished? I *did* take Lysa to Auntie Polina's, and I *didn't* feel guilty about it. But what if Mama, Maria, or Auntie Iryna were punished because of what I did? Maybe even killed, like Mr. Kitai and the others. I couldn't let that happen.

A beam of moonlight illuminated the outline of Mr. Kitai's eyeglasses as they rested on the night table. Mere hours ago, he had been wearing them, standing in the square with his family. His last gesture had been a courageous one. My parents' wedding portrait was in shadows, but even so, I felt my father's eyes and knew what he expected. A shiver ran through me. Two dead fathers were watching, both urging me to be brave—to protect my family.

I thought about the Commandant's wife and how I had left in such a hurry. That was certainly not brave. It wasn't smart either if I was hoping to keep the job. Add to that the problem with Marga.

There was no point in trying to sleep anymore, so I got up and dressed. I put the eyeglasses in my pocket and went to the main room. I would have loved to be able to sort through my thoughts, but I felt angry and sad and frightened and furious all at once. And I felt totally powerless and not particularly brave. It was too early to milk Krasa and it was too dark to mend or collect eggs or do other useful things.

But I *could* get our morning bucket of water. It was a small chore, not brave at all, but what a nice surprise it would be for Maria, who for once in her life wouldn't start a day by fetching water.

No one was at the pump, so it took no time to fill the pail, but as I lugged it home I had a new appreciation for my sister. My hands ached with the weight of the pail, and by the time I got home, my knees were bruised from it knocking into them. Maria might be fearful of walking Krasa the two kilometers to the pasture, but thank goodness she was, because I wouldn't last a day doing her chores.

I set the pail down in front of our door and stretched the kinks out of my back. I was about to go in when I noticed Dolik, lost in thought, sitting cross-legged on the front step of his house. I walked over and sat down beside him.

He glanced at me and nodded, but didn't say a word. We sat there silently for long minutes, with me sitting so close to him that I could feel the warmth of his breath. It wasn't necessary to ask his thoughts. I knew what they would be.

"It's not your fault," I said, reaching my hand over to his and giving it a small squeeze.

"That's easy for you to say," he murmured, pulling his hand away.

"You tried to tell me it wasn't my fault when Uncle Roman died," I told him. "You were right, but I was too upset to believe it." I reached into my pocket and drew out Mr. Kitai's eyeglasses.

He snatched them from my hand. "Where did you get these?"

"Where do you think? I had to see for myself," I said. "I was hoping that the Commandant had just tried to scare us, and that the men were still alive."

"But they weren't," said Dolik. It was a statement. "I went there too, for the same reason."

"Last night?"

He nodded.

I told him about the Volksdeutsche sorting through the clothing.

"Harvesting clothing from the dead," said Dolik. "Is that all we're worth?"

Maria was still rubbing the sleep from her eyes when I came back into the house with the water. Her face broke into a broad grin. "Thank you, Krystia. That was sweet of you."

Mama filled the kettle. "Why were you out so early, Krystia?" she asked. "I'd rather that you didn't while it's still so dark."

"We have a new problem," I said, sitting down at the table. I told them about Marga's threat. "And it's so unfair," I said, "because she only knew about the extra cow because I gave them milk."

"It was a kind act," said Mama. "Maybe another kind act will soften her opinion."

She took down a willow basket from the shelf. "Maria, can you collect the eggs? And Krystia, can you milk Krasa now, please?"

Half an hour later, Mama assembled a food basket: two fresh chicken eggs, a container of milk, plus a jar of blackberry jam and another of strawberry. "Take this to Frau Schneider and see if you can win her sympathy."

I carried the basket to Auntie Iryna's old house and tapped on the door, hoping that Frau Schneider, and not Marga, would answer.

No such luck.

Marga opened the door just a bit and stuck out her nose. "What do *you* want?"

"Is your mother home?"

"She wouldn't want to see you."

The door opened wider and Frau Schneider stood behind her daughter. "Krystia," she said, looking at the basket in my arms. "Come in."

My stomach lurched as I stepped in and realized what these two were dressed in. Marga wore the baker's white trousers and shirt. Frau Schneider wore the dogcatcher's gray shirt and brown trousers. Looking at them made me think of vultures, picking at scraps from the dead.

As I took a deep breath and stepped inside, I realized that they didn't need the items I had brought. A large sack of flour and a smaller one of sugar sat on the table. There were tinned items as well, all stamped with German labels: *Schweinefleisch, Schmalz, Kaffee.*

"I came to apologize," I said, thrusting the basket into Frau Schneider's arms.

She set it onto the table, taking the eggs out first, then

removing the cloth. "How thoughtful of you," she said, holding the jam jars up to the window light. "Milk too. I know you don't have much to share." She regarded me with a puzzled look. "What do you have to apologize for?"

"There was a cow in your shed before you arrived," I said.

"That second cow we saw you with," said Marga, crossing her arms. "You stole it from us."

"That's quite enough, Marga," said Frau Schneider. "Krystia, what is it that you'd like to apologize for?"

"This house was my aunt's, and the cow was hers too, but the Commandant forced her out and told her to leave everything in the house."

"She must have done something bad to deserve that," said Marga. "She should have done what the Commandant said."

It was hard not to be angry at Marga's words, but what good would it do? I raised my eyes to Frau Schneider's and said, "The reason my aunt was forced out is because the Commandant didn't want a whole house used by just one person when there were many refugees coming into our town. Auntie Iryna's son and husband had just been killed by the Soviets, so she was suddenly on her own." I purposely *didn't* mention Borys—still living but in hiding.

"Then you've lost family, just as we have," said Frau

Schneider, her eyes filling with tears. "Where did your aunt go?"

"She's with us," I said. "The cow is in the country. I brought you eggs and milk and jam by way of apology."

"You didn't have to do that," said Frau Schneider. "But how kind of you to think of us."

Marga's expression was hard to read. Would she still tell the Commandant about us? I took a deep breath and forced myself to be brave. "If you or Marga told the Commandant what we did, we could be punished."

"My dear girl," said Frau Schneider, "I would never say such a thing to the Commandant. You were so kind to us when we first came to town, offering us milk, and now coming here and telling us outright about the cow. That takes courage. It doesn't matter, anyway, because I wouldn't want my daughter out on her own to take a cow to pasture while there's a war on. And the Volksdeutsche Liaison Office acts like a welfare agency, supplying us with all that we need."

I thought back to the day before. The uniformed man organizing the newcomers to dig the grave pits, organizing them to sort the clothing. *This* was their welfare agency? To watch as others were killed and then steal their things?

Marga remained silent as her mother spoke, but her brow was furrowed.

"What about you, Marga?" I asked. "Do you forgive my family for taking the cow and chickens?"

She didn't respond.

Frau Schneider regarded her daughter. "You wouldn't bring this up with the Commandant, would you, Marga?"

Marga stared down at the dirt floor and her face flushed pink. "No, Mutter, I wouldn't," she finally said.

"Good," said Frau Schneider. She looked from her daughter to me. "Shake hands, girls," she said. "We're in the midst of war, but all the more reason for human kindness."

I reached out my hand and gripped Marga's, but she gave me a quick, limp handshake in return.

I was about to leave, but Frau Schneider put her hand on my forearm. "I have something for you."

She took a tin of pork from the kitchen table and placed it in my basket. "Thank you, Frau Schneider," I said. "That is most generous of you."

As I walked home, I puzzled over the enigma that was Frau Gertrude Schneider. It was thoughtful of her to give us pork, and good to make Marga promise to keep our secret from the Commandant, yet it was not a kind woman I had seen the day before, coldly sorting through the clothing of murdered Jews. And it wasn't a kind woman who could so easily wear the clothing of the dead. I would step lightly around Marga—and also Frau Schneider.

Mama was thrilled with the pork, and relieved at the kindness behind it. This pork was too precious to use up now, so I hid it, thinking of the future.

I regarded the worried faces around our table. It was less than a week since the execution of the hundred and one Viteretz Jews. My whole family was here—Borys, Uncle Ivan, Auntie Iryna, Maria, Mama, and me. And in my heart I felt the presence of Tato, Uncle Roman, and Josip.

"They've arrested our Ukrainian leaders in Lviv," said Uncle Ivan slowly. "Our independence is dead."

Mama put her hand to her heart. "This is the end of us all, then."

"I refuse to believe that," said Borys. "This country doesn't belong to Stalin, and it doesn't belong to Hitler! Even without our leaders, we'll do what we can to resist."

His words scared me a little, but also made me proud. "Are *you* in danger?" I asked.

Borys looked at his cup of tea but didn't reply.

"Yes, we're in danger," said Uncle Ivan.

"Uncle Ivan," I said, looking at him but also at Borys, "I could keep my eyes and ears open for information when I'm cleaning at the Commandant's. Officers sometimes come to the house when he's there, to give him information."

Mama glanced at me and then nodded. "I can do that as well, and so can Maria."

Maria looked startled by the idea, but she didn't argue.

Uncle Ivan nodded ever so slightly. "Thank you."

CHAPTER ELEVEN
BAD THINGS COME

By midsummer, the Commandant must have felt that he had complete domination of our town, because he sent most of his soldiers to the front in the East. In their place came a group of German administrators: office workers, managers, nurses, doctors, teachers, and police.

These new people were quite different from the Volksdeutsche refugees who had already settled in after arriving on the heels of the army. These ones weren't starving and ragged. They wore good clothing and spoke in a cultured way, and seemed to be on friendly and familiar terms with one another. It seemed that they had worked together as a team before coming to Viteretz.

They were also different from the military, which was nearly all men. This new group included a surprising number of female teachers, nurses, and office workers. From the snippets of conversation I was able to hear at the house, I realized that these new people were true Nazi believers.

And what *did* the Nazis believe?

I pieced it together from bits of their conversations. The Nazis had a complicated way of putting people into categories. The Commandant used different terms to describe the various groups. The ones who were considered good were called Aryan, German, and Volksdeutsche. These were part of something the Commandant called the Master Race. The Nazis thought everyone else was "subhuman."

I witnessed the actions of one true believer with my own eyes as I was walking Krasa to a farm in the country to be bred—we hoped she'd get pregnant so she would continue to give milk for another year.

This woman wore a white cloth over her hair and a white smock over a light blue dress. It wasn't until I was closer that I saw the armband with the red cross on it and realized she was a nurse. She had set up a first-aid station on a horse-drawn wagon, and she was slowly making her way down the street, looking after the medical needs of the refugees. She dressed an infected eye for an elderly man and gave some sort of needle to another, then she rocked a crying baby in her arms as she carried on an animated conversation with the mother. She seemed to be very good at her job—that is, for those she considered part of the Master Race.

A lineup of Volksdeutsche had formed, but a young boy wearing a skullcap approached her. He cradled his forearm, which seemed to be resting at an odd angle. His face was smudged with dirt and there was a rip in the knee of his trousers.

"How did you hurt your arm?" asked the woman.

"I, ah . . . tripped," said the boy.

"It looks more like you've been beaten."

The boy didn't say anything, but his face flushed red and he reluctantly nodded.

"I can't help you," she said. "You're Jewish."

"But my arm . . ." he said. "I think it might be broken."

The nurse ignored him and walked over to the teenage girl who was next in line.

Anger boiled up inside me. Didn't nurses take a pledge to help everyone who needed it? How would she feel if the tables were turned and it was her own son who needed help?

The boy walked away, now in tears.

"Excuse me," I said as I stepped alongside him. "Go to the brown house across the road from the church." I pointed down the street.

He looked up at me, confused.

"There's a lady doctor there. A *Jewish* lady doctor. She'll set your arm for you, I know for sure."

"Thank you," he said.

I felt helpless and angry as I watched him walk toward the Kitai house. The boy had been denied care for no reason except that he was Jewish. Was this kind of thing happening in other towns as well?

With all the crystal, paintings, and silver arriving at the Commandant's house, Frau Hermann kept me busy with dusting and polishing. These were easy chores that I did in silence, with the Commandant and his wife hardly noticing my presence. I often overheard snippets of Frau Hermann's telephone conversations. They were mostly about luncheons and clothing and flowers. Herr Commandant wasn't home much, as he had an office in the municipal building next door and his job took him other places as well. But when he was home, the bits I heard of his phone calls were troubling—about bullets, barbed wire, and the front.

I also learned that the Soviets and Britain were now on the *same* side of the war, fighting the Nazis together. This made no sense. Surely the British knew that the murderous Soviets were not much different from the Nazis? Couldn't the British fight them both?

One morning in August I noticed the Commandant's uniform jacket hanging on a hook by the entrance, with the edge of what looked like a telegram sticking out of the pocket. I looked around to be sure I was alone, then slid it out to read. The Nazis were nearly all the way to Leningrad. I thought of all the towns and villages between here and Leningrad. If people like the Commandant were in charge of all those other towns, I could picture the mass graves and the shootings there. Who would be left alive by the time these two horrible armies were finished?

The sound of Frau Hermann's clicking heels startled me from my thoughts. I returned the telegram to the Commandant's pocket and continued with my dusting. The Commandant's wife bustled into the room. She was in high spirits, perhaps because she knew about the Nazis' success in the war, but also because she was arranging a party for the newly arrived true believers who had come from the Reich to help with the running of our town.

Mama and I worked very hard on the day of the party. I was supposed to be keeping up with the dirty dishes in the kitchen, but at the last minute one of the Volksdeutsche serving maids became ill.

Frau Hermann came into the kitchen and surveyed all of us who were frantically cleaning pots, polishing wine glasses, and arranging food on trays.

"You," she said, pointing at me. "You're the same size as Wilma. You'll have to take her place."

She took me to a room beside the kitchen and pointed to a neatly pressed uniform draped across the back of a chair. "Put that on," she said. "And tie your hair up. You'll also need to wear those." She indicated a pair of sturdy-looking leather shoes. "Hurry and dress, then go find Helga and she'll tell you what to do."

I would have much preferred to stay in the kitchen, rather than wearing someone else's clothing and doing a job that I had never done before. What would the Commandant's wife do if I made a mistake? But then again, the party might be a good opportunity for me to learn something that could help us stay alive. I'd have to be brave.

I slipped out of my own clothing and put on the black skirt and blouse, then tied the white apron over the top, but when I slipped my foot into the first shoe, I realized they were too small. I curled in my toes and tied the laces loosely, but with each step they pinched.

When I found Helga, she redid my hair and adjusted the apron. "You'll have to do," she said, frowning. "I wouldn't trust you with the drinks tray, but perhaps you'll be steady enough to pass around this one."

She handed me a silver platter laden with small open-faced sandwiches. They all looked delicious. Each small sandwich contained more food than I had eaten all day.

I balanced the heavy tray in front of me and watched as the guests shoved the tidbits into their mouths as they kept talking and laughing. I was certain that none of the guests saw me as anything more than a walking tray, and that was fine with me.

The snippets of conversation were mostly about the weather or life back home. There were a couple of conversations about Leningrad, and also something called "the Hunger Plan." But the phrase that surfaced more frequently was "the Jewish Question."

What did that mean? The way these Nazis talked, it was a *problem* for them, not a question.

By the time the party was over, my shoulders ached from holding the tray, and when I took off the shoes, my socks were stained with blood. I put my own clothing back on and went to the kitchen to help Mama finish up with the cleaning.

There was a mound of half-eaten sandwiches left over. "We're not supposed to take any of this," said Mama, but she and the rest of us filled our pockets. "What the Commandant doesn't know won't hurt him."

That night, as I soaked my bloodied feet in a basin of cool water, Mama, Maria, Auntie Iryna, and I feasted on the leftovers. I had a stomachache all night but I didn't care.

CHAPTER TWELVE
THE JEWISH QUESTION

It was a hot day in August when Auntie Iryna and her chickens disappeared. At first I was frantic, thinking she had been taken or killed, but then I remembered that Borys had wanted her to go to the forest with him. I asked Mama, and she said, "Yes, that's where Iryna is."

I tried to picture her living in the forest, sleeping on a mattress of fir boughs with her chickens by her side, but I couldn't see it.

"Iryna's stronger than you think," said Mama, almost as if she guessed my thoughts.

I had apparently done a good enough job at the party that Frau Hermann trusted me to act as a maid whenever Wilma was busy. To save my toes and the socks, I'd wrap my feet tightly with thin cotton strips before pulling on the socks.

It turned out that Frau Hermann and her friends were hardly worth eavesdropping on. They talked about silly things like dresses and cake recipes. Didn't they know that we were in the middle of a war? What I really wanted to hear about was the Jewish Question. Dolik and Leon and Doctor Mina would want to know, so they could prepare. So would Nathan and his parents.

Most evenings, Mama, Maria, and I would talk about the things we'd overheard, and try to put it all together. It was obvious that all the people considered "subhuman" by the Nazis were treated poorly, but the Commandant didn't talk about the Subhuman Question, only the Jewish Question. What was the question?

At the end of August, we got an inkling.

Flyers were posted throughout Viteretz demanding that Jews wear distinctive armbands—a blue Star of David painted on a white piece of cloth. As I walked through town seeing all the people forced to wear them, it chilled me knowing that everyone who was a part of the Commandant's Jewish Question was now clearly identified.

At first Dolik refused to wear his. "It would make me feel like a prisoner," he said.

But then a Polish man whose father had been Jewish was caught by the police and shot dead in the street for not wearing one.

"He wasn't even *Jewish*," said Dolik. "Didn't he go to St. Joseph's?"

"But his *papers* identified him as Jewish," I said. "Just like yours do. The Nazis are stopping people on the street, demanding to see our papers. You *have* to wear the armband or you'll be shot."

As a warning to all, the man's body was left in the middle of the road to rot in the heat. A full week went by before the new Volksdeutsche dogcatcher loaded the bloated body into the back of his wagon and took it away.

After that, even people who had just one Jewish grandparent began wearing the armband so they wouldn't be shot. But while Jews *not* wearing them could be shot, Jews *wearing* the armbands were forced into labor. The official order was that any Jew between the age of fourteen and sixty had to perform labor, but Leon and Dolik were both younger than fourteen. Still, they often joined the work crews. "We decided it was safer to be considered useful to the Nazis," Dolik explained to me.

It seemed that nearly every day, a different group of Jews would be summoned at a moment's notice. Sometimes they were made to do manual labor like renovating our school for its new German students or rebuilding bombed houses. At other times, a few would be selected to perform pointless and humiliating tasks. Once, the Segal family was made to collect the horse dung from the streets with their bare hands and dispose of it in the Jewish cemetery. It was a blasphemous and horrible job, and it was especially hard on Mrs. Segal, whose weak leg left her exhausted at the best of times.

Leon, Dolik, and other young Jews were given wheelbarrows, pickaxes, and shovels and marched out to widen the dirt road beyond town. Day after day, the same group was called, and each day they had to travel farther to complete their task. They wouldn't get back until dark.

One evening I sat with Dolik on our front step after he got back from a grueling day of road widening. His hands were a blistered mess and his face was still covered in dirty sweat. "I've never done this kind of labor before," he said. "I'm not very good at it."

"At this rate, you're going to collapse from exhaustion," I said.

"But if I'm useful, I'm safer," said Dolik.

A few days after this conversation, things did improve slightly. I noticed that Dolik and his brother weren't being sent out every *single* day to work on the roads. Sometimes they were given less arduous jobs around town, like picking up trash or sweeping the sidewalks.

"Maybe the Nazis are realizing the work will be of better quality if they treat their workers more humanely," I said to Dolik as we sat side by side on his front step.

"That's not it," he said. "Some of the leaders in our community offered to take over the management of the work groups. They've formed what the Commandant calls a *Judenrat*. There's still the same amount of work, but the *Judenrat* is able to assign it more fairly than the Nazis."

It was a small improvement, but a welcome one.

CHAPTER THIRTEEN
ROOT CELLAR

As summer turned to fall, we had one piece of excellent news: Krasa was pregnant and her calf would be born in mid-April. Her milk would start to dry up around January and she'd likely be completely dry for February and March, but once her calf was born, we'd have plenty of milk again, plus we'd have a calf to sell.

In addition to our usual chores and the job of cleaning at the Commandant's, we harvested our potatoes, cabbages, and onions from the garden and stored them in our root cellar. We had just taken down the last of the potatoes when a woman from the Volksdeutsche Liaison Office came to the house.

"Your produce," she said, writing notes on her clipboard. "Where is it?"

"Harvested," said Mama. "And stored for the winter."

The woman tapped her clipboard with the tip of her pen. "Your produce is needed for the war effort."

"We have only a small garden," said Mama. "And we'll barely have enough to get through the winter as it is. If you take our produce, we'll starve."

"That is no concern of mine," said the woman. "Now please show me into your root cellar."

"And what would happen if we don't show it to you?" asked Mama.

"You do not want to test me on that," said the woman.

Mama opened her mouth to say something else, but then closed it again. As we walked around to the back of the house, the woman noticed our chickens. "How many?" she asked.

"Two," I said, gulping.

"Any cows?"

"One," said Maria.

The woman noted that on her clipboard, then looked up, frowning. "So it's a mother and two daughters who live here, that's it?"

Mama nodded.

"That one can show me the root cellar," she said, pointing to me.

I opened up the double wooden doors and stepped

down the rickety ladder into the cellar, all the time trying to control my anger. Maybe this horrible woman would fall down our ladder and break her neck. But if that happened, would we be punished?

I swallowed back my anger and steadied the woman's elbow so she wouldn't slip. I forced myself to be calm as she checked our shelves with a flashlight and wrote the inventory on her clipboard. She kicked at the dirt floor in a number of places and knocked on the walls. I had buried the can of pork from Frau Schneider in the floor, but the woman didn't find it.

"You can't keep any of what's in this cellar," she said to Mama once she stepped out. "But since you are widowed with two daughters, I'll let you keep your cow and chickens."

Mama's face went a pasty white, but she managed to say, "Thank you."

I watched in stunned silence as the woman jotted a few more things on her clipboard, then put her pen away. Was *this* the Hunger Plan, to take food away from us so that we died? I thought of the coming winter—how would we possibly get through it?

As the woman stood there, Volksdeutsche workers with a horse-drawn wagon arrived. She directed them to our cellar and we watched helplessly as they loaded up all our food.

The woman turned and was about to leave, but then hesitated. At first I thought she might change her mind and let us keep some of our produce, but she said to Mama, "You should send one of your girls to work in Germany."

Mama's mouth was set in a grim line and her knuckles were clenched white. "Why would I do that?" she asked.

"Your daughter would be fed and paid. She could send money home."

It took Mama a moment to answer. "Thank you for the suggestion."

When the woman left, Mama turned to us and said, "I don't believe her. You see how badly they treat us here. Why would they treat us any better in Germany? They will *not* defeat us."

I thought about Mama's words as I walked Krasa to the pasture that evening. I was determined to be as brave as Mama. I would not let the Nazis defeat me, but I just wished they had left us with a bit more food.

At least we still had Krasa and the chickens. We could still sell some of the milk while we had it, and we could sell eggs. With the money from that, we could buy potatoes from Auntie Polina and her neighbors.

With our food gone, working for the Commandant became even more important. He didn't pay us much, but the small amount we did get could mean the difference between living and starving.

I led Krasa to graze at Auntie Iryna's pasture and stood on the high rock, looking into the distance. The newly widened road stretched toward Lviv. It had been so easy for the Nazi and Soviet armies to invade us even with narrow roads, but now we were wide open for destruction.

I shaded my eyes and squinted at the farms surrounding Viteretz. Soldiers were guiding teams of farmers to harvest, just like they used to under the Soviets. And just like then, the produce was being loaded into trucks and driven away. They were confiscating the farmers' produce as well?

My stomach did a sick flip. What would our *farmers* live on? And what would they have left to sell to us towns-folk? This was a disaster. Money can't buy food that doesn't exist. *Everyone* but the Nazis would be hungry this winter. How would we get through February and March and half of April without even milk?

When I got back with Krasa I told Mama and Maria what I'd seen.

"They will *not* defeat us," said Mama, her eyes welling with tears. "We can forage for wild roots and plants."

"Will we still be able to sell some of the milk and eggs?" I asked.

"Our neighbors will need that food from us," said Mama. "Although we will need it too. We'll sell some milk, but we'll have to make more cheese than usual, so we can store it."

Throughout this exchange, Maria sat quietly, but a big tear fell onto the table. "We're going to starve in the spring," she said, wiping her eye with the back of her hand. "If I were brave enough, maybe I'd go to Germany like the woman suggested. I could send money back to you and Krystia."

"No," said Mama. "I want my daughters here with me. Let's just try to get by one day at a time. The rest is up to the grace of God."

CHAPTER FOURTEEN
THE FALCON'S CALL

Maria had taken to walking Krasa to the pasture with me in the evenings. This was partly because Mama was now worried about me being alone at dusk, as the Nazis were showing their true faces. But also because Maria wanted to. This was a big decision for her, and I was so proud of my little sister. It was also nice to have the company.

I would hold on to Krasa's tether and Maria would walk in front, spying out anything useful on the road or in the ditch. She would occasionally find a stray hen's egg, but also some items that had fallen off the trucks and carts of the people coming into town. A baby's rattle or someone's cane didn't interest her, but once Maria found a coil of dried sausage; another time she found a dented tin of sardines.

Along the way she'd tell me things she didn't want to say in front of Mama, like how she hated working at the Commandant's.

"I hate it too," I told her. "But working there probably saves us from worse jobs. Besides, we can sometimes hear useful things."

Once we'd get to the pasture and Krasa was grazing, we'd look for mushrooms, berries, nettles—anything that could be eaten. And it was nice to have two sets of eyes for this. We'd also play games, like seeing who could jump the farthest and who could run from one end of the pasture to the other without tripping.

One evening as Krasa munched on parched grass in our pasture, and Maria and I searched for edible shoots and roots, a shadowy figure appeared in the bushes. My heart nearly stopped beating.

"It's okay, Krystia. It's just me."

"Borys?"

I ran to hug my cousin. He picked me up and twirled me around, just like he used to when we were younger. I breathed in his scent of smoke and tree sap and realized how much I missed having him around.

"It's good to see my favorite oldest cousin," he said, putting me back on the ground.

"What about me?" said Maria with mock indignation.

"You're my favorite *youngest* cousin," he said, pinching her cheek.

He bent his knees until we were all eye level. "Let's

have a staring contest. I know I'll win, because girls blink more than boys do."

This was a game we had played as children, and it was *Borys* who usually blinked first. The trick to winning was to squint a little bit so your eyes didn't get dry. I put my hands on my hips, squinted just enough, and stared him down. Maria had a different method—kind of cheating, but Borys always let her do it. She'd hold her eyelids up with her fingers. For a full minute, Maria and I stared into Borys's eyes. I counted to sixty without blinking.

Then, instead of blinking, Borys closed his eyes slowly, then opened them again.

"Why did you do that?" I asked.

"A gift to my favorite cousins," he said, tugging on one of my braids. "I maintain my perfect losing streak from childhood."

"You are silly," I said, punching him lightly in the stomach. "I would have won anyway." Maria grabbed one of his arms and tickled him in the ribs.

"Stop," he said in mock protest. "I'm going to tell Mama that Krystia and Maria are beating me up."

We stopped tickling him. "Is she in good health?"

"Mama is fine," he said. "And I'm glad for her company. You'd be amazed at how quickly she's settling in.

And speaking of Mama," he said, reaching down for a sack that we hadn't noticed on the ground, "she asked me to bring you these."

Maria took the sack from him and opened it up. *Pidpenky*—honey mushrooms. "Are you sure you can spare these?" she asked. "No one has extra food these days."

"Things are going to get worse before they get better," said Borys.

"Can they *get* much worse?" I asked.

Borys didn't answer, but looked lost in his own thoughts. Then he said, "I need you girls to do something."

"Anything."

"The Segals have photographs for us." He led us a few steps into the bushes, then crouched down beside a big rock, brushing away loose leaves and dirt to reveal a buried metal pot, lid and all.

"Someone will try to come by here about once a day," said Borys. "Sometimes there will be a package in here for you to take back to the Segals."

"We can do that," said Maria. "And this is all secret, right?"

Borys nodded. "You can't talk to *anyone* about this."

He wrapped one arm loosely around my shoulder and another around Maria. "Stay safe, dear Cousins. I worry about you."

As he turned to disappear back into the brush, Maria caught his hand. "I have a favor to ask of you."

He looked at her. "Anything," he said.

"Take us to your encampment in the forest."

His eyes widened slightly at the suggestion. "That's a good idea," he said. "There may come a time when you need to get there."

"Why don't we go with you now?" I asked.

Borys shook his head. "If we left now, you'd end up bringing the cow home in the dark, and that could raise suspicions. Come to the pasture early tomorrow. I'll be waiting for you."

We got to the pasture about an hour earlier than usual. I tied Krasa with a loose tether so she could still graze but wouldn't wander out onto the road.

Borys stepped out of the shadows and motioned to us to follow him. He led us on a meandering route through a patchwork of pasture and farmland, hiding in the shadows of trees and large rocks. Pasture changed to woods and forest, and Borys would pause every once in a while to point out a landmark. Sometimes it would be an oddly shaped tree or a curve in a stream—always so subtle you'd miss it if you didn't know what you were looking for.

Then Borys stopped altogether. He held up his hand to make sure that we kept still as well. He took a deep breath and made the call of the falcon: *kak kak kak.*

He stood perfectly still and waited. I grabbed Maria's hand and we waited too. Five minutes passed.

A girl who looked to be just a few years older than me appeared from the shadows. She wore a peasant skirt and a Soviet army jacket, and had a rifle slung across her back. She nodded to Borys, then asked him, "Who are you?"

"I'm Borys Fediuk."

"Why are you here?"

"These are my cousins, Maria and Krystia Fediuk. They're working with us and they need to know how to get to our encampment."

"What is the answer to the question?"

"Ukraine is not yet dead."

The girl nodded again. "Follow me in." She signaled to people I couldn't see, likely to tell them to hold their fire. I thought it was smart that she'd asked Borys those questions, even though it was obvious she knew who he was. If we were enemies and he was our prisoner, he could have intentionally answered wrong and *she* would know, but the enemies wouldn't catch on.

The encampment looked like uninhabited forest, and neither Maria nor I could detect any people. We followed

Borys through a narrow opening in the brush. He moved aside a patch of sod to reveal an opening in the ground.

"There's a rope ladder," he said. "Follow me down."

"Oh my," said Maria, once her eyes had adjusted to the dimness. "Is this where people sleep?"

We were in a long underground room. Some natural light filtered in through overhead grates covered with branches. Along both sides of the room were narrow cots, three deep. A rough wooden table with benches on either side took up the middle. Rifles in various stages of repair were on the table.

"We've been stealing those weapons and stockpiling them," said Borys.

"Is Auntie Iryna here?" I asked.

"She's on a scouting mission, as is your uncle Ivan."

Borys took us back out into the daylight. "All through this area we have hidden rooms like that one," he said. "There are similar encampments all over Ukraine. We're in some disarray now, with our leaders imprisoned, but we will never give up until we drive the invaders out."

He made me and Maria find the way back to our pasture, but he kept us in sight to make sure we didn't get lost. It encouraged me to know that we were doing what we could to fight back against the Nazis. But would it make a difference?

That night as I tried to get to sleep, I thought about the encampment and the secret codes that the insurgents had used. The national symbol of Ukraine was the *Tryzub*, which to some people resembled a trident, but to me it always looked like a falcon in flight. I guess it did to Borys and his friends too, and that's why they used the *kak kak kak* of the falcon as their code. And the phrase about Ukraine not yet being dead? That was a line of a popular song from before the war. If we had our own country, that song could be its anthem. I hoped and prayed that the sentiment of the song was true.

And I would do my part to fight back, even though right now all that meant was delivering packages and photographs between the insurgents and the Segals.

A few days went by with no photographs from the Segals, but then Mrs. Segal slipped an envelope into my skirt pocket as I handed her a bottle of milk.

When I got home, I took out the photos. I thought the Segals might have taken secret pictures of the mass execution, or of all the food being confiscated—proof of Nazi crimes against civilians to send to foreign newspapers. But instead these were boring portraits of people from around town. There was one of their son, Nathan, and another of Leah Steinburg, the dogcatcher's widow. Most seemed to be of young men who were nearly old enough to be in the army, but none were of the Nazis. What was so special about *these* photos?

I put them back into the envelope and pushed them into my skirt pocket so I wouldn't forget to take them to the drop-off spot in the pasture.

CHAPTER FIFTEEN
THREE SMOOTH STONES

In order to make our food last longer, we started to skip the midday meal. Breakfast would be milk plus whatever we could find growing wild—grasses, crab apples, sorrel, roots.

Supper was milk or cheese, or an egg if the chickens had laid any, plus the wild things we foraged and made into a soup. After a week, I learned to ignore the pangs of constant hunger.

There were a few apple and pear trees out toward the country, but those were stripped bare by other hungry people. Auntie Iryna twice left a package of mushrooms at the hiding spot in the pasture, and once some nuts. I couldn't imagine how hard it must be to live in the forest and survive on just what you could find there. Her generosity brought me to tears.

Frau Hermann knew we were starving, but it didn't seem to bother her, except for the fact that we might steal food from her. Her solution was to ban Slavs from working in the kitchen. Now it was just Volksdeutsche, and they already had all the food they wanted, so they weren't tempted to steal more. I still had to carry trays of food, though, and it nearly drove me mad seeing meat and cheese and buns, and smelling them all. Frau Hermann's breath reminded me of freshly buttered bread.

One morning in mid-September I opened the drop-off tin in the pasture and found a folded paper packet. It wasn't my business—I knew that—but I was curious. So as Krasa munched, I sat on a rock and opened it up.

A stack of folded *Kennkarten* and passports. I flipped through the identification sheets. They all seemed just like the documents that I had seen people in town carrying since the Nazis had arrived. These ones were all blue, which was the color used to identify Ukrainians. I paused when I saw Nathan Segal's picture staring up at me. In the spot where it should have said his name, it read *Bohdan Sawchuk*, one of the Ukrainians who had been tortured to death by the Soviets.

Why would Nathan need a passport with *Bohdan*'s name on it? And why was his paper blue instead of yellow?

Had Uncle Ivan printed these on his hidden press? Were all of the documents falsified? He and the Segals must be working together, but what were they planning? I folded Nathan's paper back up and put all of the documents into my pocket.

When I got back into town, a crowd of people were pushing and shoving in front of the church, trying to read a notice that had been posted on the door. Valentina Zhuk extricated herself from the crush of people and met up with me. "It's not good," she said. "We've been ordered to assemble at the town square today at noon."

The thought of assembling again was terrifying. What had the Commandant planned *this* time?

It felt as if the forged documents were burning a hole in my pocket, and I would have liked to walk over to the Segals' right then. Instead I went back home and loaded up the bottles of milk on my cart as usual, and delivered them in the proper order. When I got to their house, Mr. Segal opened the door.

"Krystia," he said. "Step inside, please."

As soon as the door closed behind me, I pulled the package out of my pocket and handed it to him, relieved to have that job done.

He scanned through the documents, pausing at Nathan's just as I had. "Your uncle has done a fine job with these," he said. "I should have more photographs for you in about a week."

"Why do you need these?" I couldn't help myself from asking.

"We're trying to get people out of here."

"You want your own son to *leave* you?"

"I want my son to *live*," said Mr. Segal. "If I had the means, we would all be leaving."

I thought of Mama and Maria. What should *we* do? "So you think it's better to try to escape than stay and wait for the war to be over?"

"We're all living under their Hunger Plan, but you know they have worse intentions toward us Jews," said Mr. Segal. "Your family might live through this occupation, but if even a fraction of the rumors are true, we need to get Jews out of here." He held up Nathan's new document. "With this, Nathan might live."

"I wish there were a way to speed up getting these documents, then," I said. "Can't you get me photographs more quickly?"

"The more we make, the riskier it becomes," said Mr. Segal. "Right now, we're concentrating on young men and others we think the Nazis could target first."

"I'll do anything to help you," I said.

"Thank you, Krystia," he said. "And you know that we will do what we can to help you as well."

Townsfolk and invaders slowly gravitated to the square as the town clock chimed twelve. I found a spot on the top step of the municipal building and waited there beside Mama, Maria, and Doctor Mina. Valentina and Petro Zhuk were about a meter in front of us, beside Mr. and Mrs. Segal. Up on the balcony of the Tarnowsky house, Frau Hermann stood with several of her friends.

Leon, Dolik, and Nathan had been assigned roadwork, and that made me worry. Would they be charged with treason because they didn't come to the assembly? But just as I was thinking that, I spotted their work crew arrive at the edge of the square in a dusty column. That didn't make me feel any less anxious. It would be so easy for the Commandant to crook his finger and order them killed. I said a silent prayer.

Just like the last time, the Commandant strode confidently through the crowd and planted himself in the middle of the square. In a firm voice he announced, "None of you gathered here is in danger today."

Groans of relief rippled through the clusters of people. I barely had a chance to digest this statement when he continued. "Those sentenced to death for treason today are already in my custody. They will come forward now."

The people standing close to the St. Olha Street entrance shuffled to one side at the sound of footsteps marching behind them. I stood on my toes and saw the police ushering a group of prisoners into the square. Murmurs of alarm arose from the crowd as the policemen positioned themselves in the middle of the square, then stepped aside to reveal their captives.

Disheveled men and women, in ripped and ragged clothing, hands tied behind their backs. One was a girl with a peasant skirt and Soviet army jacket—the same girl who had met us at the encampment.

"They've captured our Ukrainian insurgents," whispered Mama.

And then I saw Borys.

I lunged forward, trying to push through the crowd. They could *not* kill Borys. I would not let them. But Mama wrapped her arms around my waist. "No, Krystia! Be quiet," she hissed. "You cannot save him."

"Let me go," I shouted, trying to break free. "I need to get to him."

Borys's head jerked up at the sound of my scream. Our eyes met. He closed his eyes slowly, then opened them again, still looking at me, like in our staring game. I knew it was his way of saying good-bye. I flailed and pulled and tried to get out of Mama's grip, but she held me firm.

The energy drained out of me and I leaned into Mama, willing myself to be still. "Borys, dear Borys," I whispered under my breath. "You cannot die."

I searched the faces of the other prisoners. Uncle Ivan had *not* been captured. Auntie Iryna had *not* been captured. I was thankful that they had been spared. But so many of the insurgents had been rounded up.

The Commandant paced in front of the group, then glared out toward the crowd. "These thirty-two men and women are guilty of anti-German activity." He motioned to a couple of policemen. They stepped forward, carrying a large canvas bundle. "Open it," he ordered.

The police revealed a collection of handguns and rifles. "These were stolen from Germans in an act of treason," said the Commandant. "We know they are collaborating with the Jews."

He turned to the police. "Take these traitors now."

Mama gripped me as the police marched the prisoners out of the square and down St. Olha Street. When the Commandant had executed our Jews, it had been done in the woods beside the Jewish cemetery. Were these prisoners being taken to the woods beside the Ukrainian cemetery? Ours was behind the Church of St. Mary. That would mean Borys would be murdered nearly across the street from our house.

Those assembled did not move and did not speak. The silence lasted for long minutes. Then all at once, the stillness was shattered by a violent crack of bullets from a few blocks away. The crowd erupted in sobs and screams.

Mama and Maria and I clung to one another and wept. Poor Auntie Iryna. Would she even *know* that Borys had been killed?

As the crowd dispersed, I walked with my sister and mother in numb silence, but when we got to our house, I couldn't bear to go in. I crossed the road to the church instead and stepped into the cool darkness. I lit a candle and said a prayer for Borys and for the others who had been so brutally killed. I stayed there so long that the candle sputtered and died in a pool of wax. My throat was raw from weeping. When I finally stumbled out, it was nearly dusk. I had to go to Borys, to honor his memory.

I walked slowly through the graveyard to get to the wooded area. On my way, I stopped at the two fresh wooden crosses marking where Uncle Roman and Josip were buried. I searched through the earth and found two stones. I placed one on the shoulder of each of the crosses, then chanted under my breath the *Vichnaya Pamyat*. "Dear Uncle and

Cousin," I said, tears streaming down my face, "I remember and love you."

I walked into the woods and easily found the fresh pile of dirt covering the newest mass grave. The Volksdeutsche with their shovels were gone. It was just me and the souls of the newly dead. I fell to the ground and scrabbled around with my hands until I found a smooth round stone.

I approached the mound and knelt in front of it, placing my stone at the edge and praying for Borys and all our insurgents. How long did I stay there, kneeling and weeping? Mama came and found me. She helped me to my feet and we stumbled home together.

That night in bed, Maria and I clutched each other and wept. I thought of that false passport with Nathan's photograph and Bohdan's name on it. All the people in today's mass grave were Ukrainian. How much protection would a false Ukrainian passport get Nathan?

CHAPTER SIXTEEN
A KILOGRAM OF GOLD

When I was little, Tato told me the story of a frog that was put in a pot of cool water. The pot was put on the stove to simmer, but it heated so gradually that the frog didn't realize it was being cooked until it was too late. That's how I felt about the Commandant and his plans for Viteretz. Each of his actions was worse than the last, but then we adjusted.

Gnawing hunger was now normal. People forced into sudden heavy labor was normal. "Subhumans" killed on a whim was normal.

We usually started back to school in September, but the Nazis believed that we "subhumans" only needed enough education to understand their orders, so the schools were closed to us beyond grade four. Anya, the priest's wife, taught us secretly, but we still had heavy labor and all our chores to do, so learning became hard to fit in.

It made me sick to look at the Commandant or his wife, but whenever I was working in their house, I pasted a smile onto my face, dusting and polishing the pretty things I knew they had stolen from their victims. I listened in on conversations whenever I could, hoping to find out something that might help us stay alive.

Our old school had been repaired and painted by labor groups, and was now used by the children of the Germans and Volksdeutsche who administered our town. In the nice weather we'd often see them in their Hitler Youth uniforms singing Nazi songs or marching down the street. Marga was a student there. I'd sometimes pass her coming home in the afternoon, looking uncomfortable with her hair twisted into tight blond braids and her uniform so heavily starched that the collar made a red mark on her neck.

The warehouse beside the school was the supply depot for the Volksdeutsche Liaison Office, where the food that had been taken from us was stored. It was also where the clothing and items taken from the executed were kept. As I watched endless wagonloads of goods arriving at that warehouse, it made me wonder if this same thing was happening in every town and city that had been conquered by the Nazis. I dreamed of breaking in and opening the doors wide, so that the stolen food and goods could be given to those who needed them so desperately.

The Nazis acted as if we needed lots of police, yet it seemed that their job was to terrorize us, not to provide law and order.

The police who most frightened me were the ones in gray-green uniforms. They came from Germany and they had guns. It was police like these who had executed Borys and our insurgents. There were uniformed Volksdeutsche as well, who also had guns. And Nazis had formed local groups of auxiliary police, so we had Polish, Ukrainian, and Jewish police who wore armbands instead of uniforms. Some of the Ukrainian and Polish police carried guns, but the Jewish police didn't—only batons.

Even walking on the street became hazardous. Once I was coming home from the Commandant's when an elderly Volksdeutsche man—I think he was the new postmaster—shook his cane and cursed at two young Polish women as they walked past him. I didn't know either woman's name, but I recognized one as a bakery clerk. The other looked as if she could be the clerk's younger sister. Both kept their eyes cast down as they passed the man, as if trying to ignore his harsh words. A Nazi policeman was passing just then and he stopped, looked from the women to the old man, and asked, "What did they do?"

"That one, she's a traitor," said the man, pointing at the older of the two.

The policeman pulled out his gun and shot her in the skull. She crumpled to the ground.

I stood, frozen in place, as the younger woman knelt and cradled her sister's bloodied head. "Why did you *shoot* her?" she shouted at the policeman. "She did nothing wrong." The policeman raised his gun again and shot her in the head too.

I thought maybe the man who had accused the woman would be horrified at the violence he had caused, but when I looked at his face, all I saw was a satisfied smirk.

The policeman looked at the man, then at me—the other witness to what he'd just done. He raised his gun and aimed it at my head. "Leave."

In a haze of shock, I walked right past the two dead sisters and the smirking man. When I got home, Mama held me in her arms as I wept. "I didn't help them, Mama," I sobbed. "I just stood there, watching."

"What is it you thought you could *do*?" she asked. "The women were already dead. And the policeman very nearly shot you."

Her words didn't make me feel any better. I went to the bedroom and ran my fingers over Mama and Tato's wedding portrait. Tato stared out at me, and I felt the disappointment in his eyes. He had wanted me to be brave, to do what was right, but instead I had walked away, not even saying anything to the policeman.

I clasped the portrait to my heart and lay down on the bed, not to sleep, but just to think. Mama was right—I knew that. If I had intervened, I would have been shot. But there had to be a way to fight back. We were doing what we could, but it wasn't enough.

It was nearly dusk on the last Monday of September and we needed more water. "Go with your sister, Krystia," said Mama. "I don't like either of you being out alone this late."

As we carried the water pail to the pump, I glanced over at Maria. It's funny how you can live with someone, even sleep in the same bed, but not pay attention to the subtle changes that happen over time. I hadn't really *looked* at Maria since the Hunger Plan had started. I still thought of her as my chubby-cheeked baby sister, but her face now looked almost gaunt. I glanced down at our two hands side by side, holding the water pail. They looked like leather on bone.

"Do you feel the hunger?" I asked her.

"Not usually," Maria said. "Except at night. I guess it's because there's nothing to take my mind off it then. I get up and drink some water. That usually helps."

"I wish there were something we could do to change this situation."

"Me too," said Maria. "But I feel so powerless."

When we got back with the pail, I was surprised to see Dolik, Leon, and Nathan just coming home from the labor they'd been assigned. Maria chatted with Nathan, and I met up with Dolik before he went into his house. "The police kept you working for extra hours today."

"It's to make up for time we're taking off. Tomorrow at sunset, Yom Kippur begins," he said, running his fingers through dirt-encrusted hair. "We've been given tomorrow and Wednesday off."

I knew that Yom Kippur was the holiest day of the year for Jews, and that it was mostly spent at synagogue. "It's encouraging that the Commandant has given you time for Yom Kippur," I said. "Maybe things will start to get better now."

But the next morning, another poster was nailed to the church door. This one read: *All Jewish males are ordered to report to the town square at noon today.*

Most people who weren't Jewish stayed away from the square at noon, for fear of being targeted by mistake, but I had to go. I couldn't imagine being anywhere else while the fate of my friends was at hand. Mama felt the same way and so did Maria, so we stood together with the Kitais and the Segals.

When the Commandant walked through the crowd, he paused, his eyes on Mama. His brows creased as if in thought, but he said nothing. He continued to the center of the square.

"It has come to my attention," he said, "that the Jews of Viteretz have been hoarding gold. I hereby demand one kilogram of gold to be collected from them."

This statement was met by shocked silence. The Commandant paced up and down, then stopped again. "Where is the head of my *Judenrat*?"

There was movement in the crowd just behind us and Shimon Cohen stepped forward.

"Herr Commandant," he said, his eyes fixed on the toes of Commandant Hermann's leather boots. "We are very poor in this town. I cannot imagine there being a kilogram of gold in this entire *region*, let alone Viteretz itself."

"I don't believe you," said the Commandant. "Now, Mr. Cohen, please have the forty finest Jewish men of Viteretz step forward."

Mr. Cohen's eyes widened at the order, and at first he said nothing, but I could imagine the thoughts that were going through his mind. Everyone who had been singled out in this way had ended up being murdered. Should Mr. Cohen really call up the finest Jewish men? But if he *didn't* do exactly as the Commandant ordered, would the results be even worse?

Mr. Cohen's body was shaking as he stumbled over some names. As the men came forward, even I knew that he had spared the finest. He hadn't named Mr. Segal, and he hadn't named the rabbi. The forty men he did call to the square were good citizens, but they were mostly elderly, and more than one seemed to be in very poor health.

"These do not look like your *finest*, Mr. Cohen," said the Commandant as he strutted in front of the forty doomed men. "Why, you didn't even call up Mr. Baruch, who is on the *Judenrat* with you."

He scanned the crowd again, then his eyes lit up. "There you are. Mr. Baruch, please come and join these fine men."

The crowd parted, and Mr. Baruch reluctantly came forward.

"No need to look so frightened," said the Commandant as he stepped in front of each man and gazed into his eyes. "You are just my hostages."

He gestured to a row of armed policemen who stood at attention at the back of the square. "Take these men to the city jail."

The policemen surrounded the forty-one men and escorted them away.

"Now, Mr. Cohen," said the Commandant. "I will

release those men once you have given me the kilogram of gold. You have until tomorrow, at sunset."

I don't know how he did it, but somehow Mr. Cohen collected the one kilogram of gold. People gave up their wedding rings, family heirlooms, cherished old coins. I was desperate to help, but we had no gold.

Mr. Cohen turned it over to the Commandant—all of it.

At dusk, as Yom Kippur began, the men were loaded onto trucks, driven to the outskirts of town—and shot.

CHAPTER SEVENTEEN
LEBHAFT

Throughout the fall of 1941 I felt like the world was closing in on us. The streets now bore German names. So did the stores. Even our town was no longer Viteretz. The Commandant renamed it Lebhaft. Both words meant "breezy," but the wind that blew through now was filled with fear.

When I was out on the street, I'd keep my eyes cast down whenever I passed someone who was German or Volksdeutsche. Most walked by as if I didn't exist, and that was fine with me. One exception was the new blacksmith. Often, when we passed on the street, Herr Zimmer would bow his head slightly and say under his breath, "Greetings, Fräulein Krystia."

I wondered if he could get in trouble for being so polite to a Slav, but he only greeted me that way when no one else was around.

On a chilly afternoon as I was coming home from the Commandant's, I decided on a whim to stop by the blacksmith shop.

"It's nice to see you, Fräulein Krystia," he said. "This is a good place to get warm on a cold autumn day. Come and sit." He pointed to the stool in the corner. The same stool I used to sit on to watch Tato work, so many years ago.

I perched on its edge and a sense of peace washed over me. It wasn't just the warmth of the coal fire in the forge, it was the memory of when Tato was still alive, and when there was no war.

Herr Zimmer pulled his visor down, but before he could continue his work, I said, "Thank you, Herr Zimmer."

"For what, Fräulein?"

"For treating me like a human."

He lifted his visor again and looked at me. "These Nazis," he said. "I don't agree with them."

His comment surprised me. The Nazis had given him my family's blacksmith shop. They had given him part of a house on this street as well. If he didn't agree with what they were doing, why was he going along with it?

"Excuse me, Herr Zimmer, but I have a question. It may not be a polite question."

The blacksmith smiled at that. "You want to know why *I* am here if I am not a Nazi. Am I correct, Fräulein Krystia?"

"Yes . . . That is what I was going to ask you."

"I had a blacksmith shop in a village near Chernivtsi," he said. "I also had a teenage son. My wife died long ago."

So, like Frau and Marga Schneider, Herr Zimmer was an ethnic German from Ukraine. "Is your son still at home?" I asked.

He shook his head. "The Soviets took over my shop and our house during the time of the Nazi-Soviet Pact. We were deported to the Reich. My son was drafted into the German army, and I was selected to live here. I pray every day that my son survives the war. But even more, I pray that my son does not become a Nazi."

Herr Zimmer's words hit me hard. I had been so wrapped up in my own troubles, and also so resentful of the invaders, that I had never stopped to consider that not all of them were bad. Was I just as guilty as the Nazis of judging others by things they couldn't control?

"I am sorry about your son, Herr Zimmer," I said. "And I'm sorry that you lost your home."

"Fräulein Krystia, when I look at you, I think of my son. I hope that strangers will treat him as an individual, and not by what they think he is."

As I walked home, I thought about our conversation. I *couldn't* control that the Nazis considered me a "subhuman." But what I *could* control was how *I* treated others.

Only one good thing was happening. The identity papers that Uncle Ivan and Mr. Segal had created, transforming Jews into Ukrainians, seemed to be working. As Dolik and I sat on the front step during the warmer evenings, he'd whisper to me the names of those who had escaped. Some went on foot, disappearing into the mountains, while others would trot beside a slow-moving train in the wee hours of the morning and hop on when an open car rolled by. Knowing that the documents worked gave me hope, but it also made me wonder why Dolik didn't try to leave. I knew for a fact that he and his brother both now possessed forged passports and that Doctor Mina had a false *Kennkarte*.

"Mami feels that it's safer for us here right now," Dolik told me. "The war is all around us, so how could we truly escape? Why jump from the frying pan into the fire? Plus, it's Mami's responsibility as a doctor to stay and help."

Was Doctor Mina right? Maybe our false documents gave nothing more than false hope. I could also understand why she was reluctant to leave her patients. With the brutal work schedules, starvation, and violence directed against Jews in particular, she had been kept very busy.

But deep in my heart, I felt that the false documents *could* make a difference. I continued to take Krasa to the pasture twice a day, and continued to transfer the photos and documents. Auntie Iryna usually brought the documents herself. She tried to come in the evening so Maria and I could see her in person. Like all of us, she had become thin, but she looked fierce with her hair braided tightly against her head and her blouse tucked into military trousers.

Since most of our own milk was now confiscated, I could no longer use the ploy of daily milk deliveries to get any new documents to the Segals.

It was Maria who came up with a solution. She took the packet from me and put it in her own pocket. "*I'll* take them. I see Nathan every day when he's finished work. No one should find that suspicious."

In addition to delivering the packets to Nathan, my sister also began getting up an hour early each morning to walk along the train tracks, searching for anything useful that might have fallen off the trains during the night. Mostly what she brought back were pieces of coal, but once she found a package of dried fruit that must have been dropped by a person escaping.

My little sister was growing into a very brave person.

Maria also lined up every day for the single piece of bread that our ration cards allowed each of us, but sometimes she'd come home with nothing. On other days, the bread she brought back would smell like something from the outhouse. At least we had a bit of milk and the occasional egg, plus the wild greens and roots that we foraged.

But Dolik's family had no chickens or cow. The Segals didn't either. And Jewish ration cards provided even less bread than ours. There was a black market in food—Volksdeutsche who worked at the warehouse would steal from there and sell it back to the locals—but the prices were so high that only the wealthiest could afford it.

Each day Dolik's cheeks seemed to grow hollower—a combination of his starvation diet and the heavy labor he was forced to do.

"You can't go on this way," I said to him one evening as we sat together on his front step. "There has to be a way to get more food."

"We have a little bit of money saved," said Dolik. "But we can't afford much when we buy food from the Volksdeutsche."

"What about buying it from farmers in the outlying areas who might have been able to hide some produce?"

"There's no way to get in touch with them," he said. "This armband is a red flag to the Nazis. They watch our every movement."

"Maybe I can figure something out."

After that conversation, I visited Auntie Polina and told her of the problem.

"We don't have much food either," she said. "The Nazis were thorough. But I'll see what I can do."

Auntie Polina set up a network of trusted farmers in the area, and among them they sold her the meager bits of food that they could spare—a bit of hard cheese from this one, sometimes a potato or two from that one, or a carrot from someone else. Then she'd meet me at the pasture. I paid her with money from the Segals and the Kitais. I also bought food for ourselves with the money we earned working at the Commandant's, and while this was a cheaper method than buying on the black market, the money still didn't go very far.

"I wish I could just give this food to you instead of having to make you pay," said Auntie Polina. "But the farmers need to buy seed to replace what was confiscated, or there will be no crops next year. And they have to repair the buildings and replace the tools that were stolen or destroyed by the armies."

"I know, Auntie," I told her. "I appreciate all that you're managing to do." What I didn't say is that I feared all of us would either starve or be killed if things continued as they were.

When I walked home that morning with a pocket of false documents plus three potatoes in my blouse, I witnessed a man being beaten by the police for having potatoes.

"If I find out you were giving these to Jews, I'll come back and shoot you," said the policeman as he hovered over the cowering man.

I silently stepped past them, head down and heart pounding. Would the policemen catch me next?

Once I got home and tethered Krasa, I collapsed into the corner of the shed and wept. What kind of person was I becoming that I could walk past a man being beaten and terrorized and only be glad that it wasn't me? I took the documents out of my pocket and looked at each solemn face staring back at me. I hoped and prayed that my small acts of rebellion would make a difference, that some of these people would escape and that my neighbors wouldn't starve. I took the potatoes out of my blouse and left one of them hidden behind a tin on the shelf. That would be our supper tonight. I would have to find the ideal time to sneak the second potato to Dolik. Maria would give the third to Nathan.

I climbed up to the loft and looked through what we

had stored there. Maybe I could find something to barter for food. Auntie Iryna's plates and kitchen things were up there, but they were plain and worn and only of sentimental value. We had some jars of jam and pickles that we were saving for when Krasa's milk went dry in the winter. And then I remembered the box Auntie Stefa had sent us from Toronto before the war. Had she sent something valuable to barter with? I brushed the straw off the top of the box and lifted the flaps.

An opened envelope addressed to Mama sat on top. When I pulled out the folded letter, a photograph fell out. It was a picture of Auntie Stefa, grinning, wearing a big coat with a fur-trimmed collar and standing on the steps of a modern building. She looked like Mama, except happy and well fed. I unfolded the letter and read:

Kataryna—

Eaton's had these in their bargain bin and I couldn't resist, so I bought the whole lot. Hope they're useful. But why don't you just come to Canada? I would be happy to sponsor you and your girls. There are plenty of jobs here for single women, plus Krystia and Maria would get the education they deserve! Think about it, won't you, sweet pea?

Love, your big sister Stefa

I folded the letter around the photo and put them both back in the envelope. What would our lives be like now if we lived in Canada instead of Viteretz? We'd have enough to eat, and there would be no war happening all around us. And maybe I'd get a big coat to wear. It sounded almost like heaven. But Viteretz was home, and Tato was buried in the cemetery across the road. Even so, part of me wished we were all safe with Auntie Stefa and far away from the Commandant and his Nazis. If only I could snap my fingers and make it happen.

I reached into the box to see what it was Auntie Stefa had got on sale. Flat packages of something wrapped in cellophane. I pulled one out and held it up to the light from the window. A package of ladies' silk stockings? I pulled out the next package and the next. The entire box was filled with silk stockings. How utterly useless. What farmer would want *stockings*? I packed them all away and climbed back down the ladder.

Something else that gnawed at me was Krasa's pregnancy. Would we be punished for not disclosing that she would have a calf in the spring? As each day went by and her belly got more noticeable, I was sure we would be caught. How long did we have before a policeman noticed? They would take her away, that was for sure, but would they punish just me? Or Maria and Mama as well? Added to that, Krasa's milk was drying up more quickly than we expected. It was going to be a very hungry winter.

I shared my worries with Auntie Polina the next time she came to the pasture with potatoes. "I have a solution," she said.

The following day she met me at the pasture, a dull-eyed cow in tow. "This is Yasna," she said. "Believe it or not, her name matched her personality when she was younger."

"I imagine you were very bright and pretty in your day," I murmured to the old cow, scratching her between the ears. Then I asked Auntie Polina, "Why did you bring her here?"

"We'll trade," said Auntie Polina. "I'll keep Krasa over the winter. I've got enough good hay, and she can give birth in the country. The Commandant will be none the wiser."

"But didn't Yasna stop giving milk long ago?" I asked. "We'll starve without milk."

"Yes, Yasna is dry. And Krasa will be drying up soon. Lysa too. But I'll make cheese and bring it when I can," said Auntie Polina. "And in the spring, we can swap back. Take Yasna home. She'll give you an excuse to come to the pasture to get produce from me until winter sets in. Plus, if anyone checks, you'll still have your one allotted cow."

It was a good plan. I hugged Auntie Polina with all my strength. "Thank you."

These were small victories over the enemy—the extra food so our friends wouldn't starve, and making sure we kept Krasa safe so *we* wouldn't starve—but then the Commandant circulated another notice. It was a long and detailed one. Copies were nailed to posts and buildings all over town. Doctor Mina stood beside me as we read. She was a fast reader, so she summarized it: "They're making all the Jews of Viteretz—or should I say Lebhaft—move out of their homes and crowd into this area." She pointed at a map of the city. "They're calling it the Jewish Ghetto."

The notice flapped in the wind. I held down the bottom to keep it still. Doctor Mina pointed to a grayed-out area. "That's where we're all supposed to move."

It was a bombed-out area in the oldest part of the town, between the boarded-up Old Synagogue and the town square. It used to have stores and a warehouse, but many of the buildings had fallen into disrepair even before the war. In the last two years, those buildings had been hit by artillery fire, so even the ones that still stood were not fit to live in. During the Soviet occupation, the ragged refugees who had followed the Soviets here would build campfires in the bombed-out rooms for warmth and cooking. When the Soviets fled, the refugees followed them, leaving rotting refuse and smoldering campfires in their wake. The area was uninhabitable, and it was also just two blocks long. There had to be more than a thousand Jews still in Viteretz. How could they all fit into such a tiny area?

"When do you have to move?" I asked.

"They've given us two weeks."

"Perhaps now is the time to escape," I whispered to Doctor Mina. "All of you have your papers now."

"And where would we escape to, Krystia?" she asked, throwing her arms up. "There is no safe place for Jews to go. Besides, with the food restrictions and overwork, our people will need me more than ever."

And while I nodded my agreement, I felt like weeping. Yes, there was danger in escaping, but there was danger in staying too. Being in the ghetto would make them a sitting target.

For the next two weeks, the mood of Viteretz was one of high frenzy. While most Jews were out on forced labor duty, Doctor Mina combed the area that would be the ghetto, looking for a suitable place to live.

"We found a room," Dolik told me finally. "It's on the second floor of what used to be the sugar beet warehouse."

"The three of you will all be living in a single room?" I asked.

Dolik shook his head. "That room is for us, *plus* the Segals—so six in one room. You wouldn't believe what the owner is charging us. That's why our two families have to rent it together."

The Commandant declared that each Jew was allowed to bring only a single suitcase into the ghetto. Anything left behind became property of the Reich.

"I won't be able to have a darkroom in the ghetto," Mr. Segal confided to Mama.

"But without your photographs," Mama asked, "how can Ivan make the counterfeit documents?"

"We'll still have our cameras, but it's a matter of developing the film."

"We'll take your darkroom equipment to the insurgents' bunker in the woods, then," said Mama. "And Michael, you'll have to write out very careful instructions on the developing process, so someone there can do it."

Doctor Mina's single suitcase was stuffed with just food, essential medical supplies, and cash. Dolik's and Leon's suitcases were similarly packed. All three wore as many layers of clothing as they could, with winter coats on top and pockets stuffed full. Even so, they had to leave a lifetime of possessions behind.

Doctor Mina sighed as we surveyed her second-floor office. "Look at how much of my medical supplies I'm losing."

Her office was larger than our entire small house, the shelves stuffed with hundreds of precious vials and bottles and boxes.

"We could put some of it in our loft and try to bring it to you bit by bit," said Mama. "But there will be so much left behind."

"Perhaps we should smash all this?" said Doctor Mina. "I don't want the Nazis to get it."

"What about the insurgents?" I asked. "They surely have need of medical supplies."

Doctor Mina turned to me. "That's a good idea."

The insurgents used the frenzy of the Jews' house-swapping, packing, and moving to sneak box upon box from Doctor Mina's office. Some of her supplies were stored in the church until Uncle Ivan could get them, and one box was put under our kitchen table. With a lot of subterfuge and a little bit of luck, a good portion of the precious medicines made it to the woods. One box of essential supplies stayed hidden in our loft.

During the upheaval of the move to the ghetto, a handful of Jews with false documents escaped. Some headed to Germany, the eye of the storm, posing as Ukrainian slave laborers. Others fled to the woods. But the Segals, like the Kitais, decided to stay: the Segals to help with the false documents in order to get more people out, and the Kitais so Doctor Mina could look after the sick and injured in the ghetto.

No sooner had our friends moved into their cramped quarters than the houses their families had lived in for generations were occupied by our enemy. This was well and truly becoming a Nazi town, with our neighbors all replaced, except for the Zhuks next door and the priest and Anya across the road.

Would the Nazis be watching us for unusual activity now? How would I transport documents and food without raising suspicion? And once there was snow on the ground,

I would no longer be able to use the pretext of taking Yasna to pasture.

With the closing of the ghetto gates, the Commandant decreed that Jews found outside the ghetto without permission would be shot on sight. Slavs who gave Jews food would be shot. And as if that wasn't enough of a deterrent, the Nazis posted signs all over town claiming that contact with Jews could spread disease.

CHAPTER EIGHTEEN
THE GHETTO

By the beginning of December, barbed wire was installed around the entire two blocks that were now deemed the Jewish Ghetto. There was a single gated entry at the south end, patrolled by police. No one was allowed in or out without a specific reason and the proper papers.

I hadn't figured out how I was going to pass food and documents through to Dolik and Mr. Segal if I couldn't get inside.

I hoped that my routine looked innocent to my new Nazi neighbors. Usually by late fall I would still take the cow out of the shed for fresh air twice a day, but she would be eating hay from the loft by this time, not grass in the pasture. If there was snow or ice on the ground, we stayed close to home, because I couldn't risk her slipping and breaking a leg. But this year, up until now I had still taken Yasna to the pasture twice a day so I could check for documents.

One day Auntie Polina met me at our pasture with all of the food she could scrounge. "I wish I could have brought you more," she said. "But we're all suffering. Krasa is now completely dry. If I'm able to get you anything more, I'll bring it to you."

From one pocket she drew out a hunk of cheese and a cube of lard wrapped in paper. From a pouch under her coat she brought out a small jar of sunflower oil, six shriveled apples, and a palm-sized wooden box of honeycomb. I put all the cash I had in her hands, knowing full well that in the coming months this food would be far more precious than the money. I wrapped my arms around her. "Thank you, Auntie."

I took the food back home, keeping some of it for us and hiding the rest for the Segals and Kitais. The question still remained: How would I get it to them?

Without the twice-daily trips to the pasture, it would be harder to check the hiding place for documents. And even if there were some, what would I do with them if I couldn't make it into the ghetto? Maybe if I slipped out to the pasture every ten days or so, it wouldn't raise the suspicions of our German neighbors.

Each day since the ghetto had been in place, I'd hidden across the narrow street and watched the police who guarded it, so I could figure out their routine. In the morning and at night when the gates were open and the labor crews were coming and going, there were maybe eight police on duty, but at other times there were only two. One would stay by the gate while the second would slowly patrol the perimeter of the ghetto.

After watching for three days, I knew I could count to one thousand from when the policeman rounded the corner to when he'd reappear on the other side. That was about nine minutes.

On the fourth day, I darted across the road once the policeman had turned the corner. I tugged frantically at various spots in the barbed wire, counting under my breath, looking for a section where the wire wasn't completely secured and could be pulled wide enough apart to make an opening I could step through. I found a spot between the old candy shop and a bank, then pushed the barbed wire back in place and hurried away. That took about four minutes.

Now that I knew how to get in, I had to figure out *when* to do it. Dolik lived on the second floor of the old sugar beet factory, and I knew exactly where that was in relation to the candy shop, but there was no point in me sneaking in if everyone was out doing labor. The only time I could be certain that someone would be in the room was during the night.

The next morning I got up before the sun rose and put Mama's wool coat over my skirt and blouse. Her coat was bulkier than mine and it gave me more places to hide food. In various pockets I hid the honey, three apples, a potato, a wedge of cheese, and an onion. If I got through, the Kitais and Segals would have enough food to supplement their rations for a number of days.

If I got caught . . . Well, I'd be just as dead for smuggling in a single potato, so more was better.

The street was dark and empty and my bare feet made no noise. Moving through the town square, I ducked behind the water pump as a policeman passed by. I got across the street from the ghetto and hid in the shadows, waiting for the policeman to appear on his route. When he rounded the corner, I darted across the road and quickly slipped through the gap in the barbed wire.

I nearly tripped over a ragged man sleeping on the ground, but caught my balance and felt my pockets to make sure none of the food had fallen out. Then I stepped over the man, keeping close to the wall of the old candy store. A policeman was patrolling the *inside* of the ghetto—and coming my way. I pressed myself into the shadow of the wall and tried to make myself small. He walked right past me.

The sugar beet building was just half a block away, so I walked quickly to it and pulled open the front door. The stench of sweat and disease was so powerful that it nearly knocked me over. Dozens of wheezing, coughing people huddled together all the way up the steps, many of them using their one suitcase as a pillow. Even in the darkness I saw more than one arm or foot wrapped in bloodied gauze. Like the man asleep on the street, these people must not have been able to find or afford a room in the tiny two-block ghetto. And by the smell, there was obviously no place to get clean.

I needed to look like I belonged, so I walked right in and tiptoed up the stairs, trying my best not to step on any fingers. A man roused groggily and pushed over to make room for me. I made my way down the dark second-floor hallway by feeling the wall, dodging more sleeping people crowded together.

I didn't know exactly where on the second floor the Kitais and Segals would be, so I tapped on the first door.

"What do you want?" asked a man's voice.

"I'm looking for the lady doctor," I said. "I've injured my arm."

"She's at the end of this hallway, on the left."

When I got to the proper door, I tapped firmly, then stepped in.

Moonlight streamed in through a high window, illuminating the six shapes huddled together for warmth on the bare floor. Each was dressed for winter—shoes and overcoat and all.

Dolik sat up, rubbing his eyes. "Krystia?"

I stepped over to him and knelt so we were eye level. "I've brought food," I said. "But I don't know when I'll be able to get more." I pulled the items out of my pockets and thrust them into his hands.

Nathan sat up and yawned. Leon woke up too. "You could have been shot, coming in here," said Nathan. "Or robbed, once you got inside."

"Well, I wasn't shot or robbed," I replied. "But it's risky. We'll have to think of a better way, *if* I'm able to get more food."

What we decided was that I would wait across the street on the days that I had food or documents. We agreed on four thirty in the morning as the best time, and I would only go out on the mornings when the moon was bright enough for them to see me from across the street. The six of them would rotate turns, so that someone would be at the gap in the loosened barbed wire at the appointed time.

But when was the next time I'd be able to find food to bring? If ever?

CHAPTER NINETEEN
ST. NICHOLAS AND CHANUKAH

Germans celebrate St. Nicholas Day on December 6, instead of December 19 like we Ukrainians do, and the Commandant's wife had decided to hold a party in the house for the officers' children that day. Each was to be given a small wrapped box filled with candy, and even though I was no longer allowed to work in the kitchen, I was one of the maids selected to sort the candies and wrap the boxes. My stomach grumbled painfully as I placed small pieces of chocolate and three sugar-dusted squares of Turkish delight into each of the boxes. How I wished I could pop just *one* candy into my mouth.

Frau Hermann had warned us, though. "I am keeping track of every single candy," she said, "so don't bother trying to steal it."

Later in the day I carried a tray laden with cheese and sausage slices and listened to the children's parents chatter about mundane things. As my feet pinched in the stiff leather shoes and my shoulders ached from the weight of the tray, I tried to concentrate on the threads of conversation, hoping to pick up something useful.

My ears perked up at the mention of silk stockings. A group of women, all wearing bright dresses, stood in the corner of the room discussing the best place to get stockings.

"My brother is stationed in Lemberg and he buys them on the black market for me," said a woman in green chiffon. I knew Lemberg was the German name for Lviv.

"He goes into a back alleyway to buy stockings?" asked a pink-clad woman.

"Well, not him personally. One of his Slav workers gets them."

"Ask if he can get me a couple of pairs," said a third woman.

When I got home after the party, I told Mama about what I'd heard. "We should sell the stockings—the ones from Auntie Stefa—in Lviv," I said. "There's a whole box full."

"That's not a bad idea," said Mama. "I didn't want to try selling them around here because the Nazis would just find our box and confiscate them all."

·   ·   ·

A few nights later Mama took a dozen of the stocking packages and wrapped them in a thin length of cloth. Maria and I helped her bind them to her back, winding the cloth around her waist snugly so it wouldn't show through her clothing.

"But what about your cleaning for Frau Hermann?" Maria asked.

"Krystia will have to take my shift," said Mama. "If Frau Hermann notices, tell her I have a bad cold and don't want to make her sick."

There was a light tapping at the door. Mama opened it and a young man and woman stepped in. "Girls," said Mama, "this is Tadeusz and Sofia Podorski. We will be sneaking onto the freight train to Lviv tonight. I should be back tomorrow, or the next day at the latest. Don't worry about me."

She kissed us each and was gone.

Of course we *did* worry. Once Maria and I finished our chores, we wrapped ourselves up in our comforter and lay in bed, listening for the rumbling sound of an arriving train, and willing Mama to be on it.

I didn't know the Podorskis personally, except that they were brother and sister. Their family was Polish and they had been wealthy before the war. Their father was one of the first people the Soviets killed—hanging him in the town square. Their mother had been sent to a labor camp in Siberia. What were they selling on the black market? Perhaps some jewels and antiques they had been able to hide away? As in Mama's case, it was better to trade anonymously in the big city, because otherwise their precious items would be confiscated.

I was glad that Mama was able to travel with two other people, and people who knew the black market, but I couldn't help but feel uneasy the whole time she was gone.

Three nights later she stepped into the house in the wee hours of the morning, so covered in a thin layer of coal dust that when she smiled at us, it looked like her teeth were floating in the air. Maria and I jumped out of bed and threw our arms around her, not worrying about the dust we were getting all over the place, just thankful that she was safe.

"Was the trip a success?" I asked.

"It was," said Mama. "Look what I got." She took a cloth bag from inside her blouse.

I picked it up. "Buckwheat?"

"Yes," said Mama, her white teeth grinning. She emptied one of her pockets. "I've got two big bags of it."

Buckwheat kasha was filling, and when boiled in water it expanded, so just these two bags would make many meals. We kept one of the bags for ourselves; the second was for our friends in the ghetto.

Mama woke as I was leaving to take the buckwheat there. "Wait, Krystia," she said, rubbing the sleep out of her eyes. "Where are those small hacksaws?"

"They're here," I said, reaching for them on a high shelf. "Why do you want them?"

"Take some to the ghetto," said Mama. "I overheard conversations while I was in Lviv. Something about deportations. If the Nazis start deporting Jews by train, these would come in handy."

I took two of the tiny hacksaws and slipped them into my pocket, then hugged Mama before I left.

Nathan looked at the hacksaws quizzically when I passed them through the barbed wire. "Do you really think they're going to deport us?" he asked.

"Maybe not," I said. "But Mama overheard *something* about deportations."

"With a hacksaw like this, I might be able to saw through a bolted-down window or door if the Nazis sent me away by train." He slipped them into his pocket.

I passed him the buckwheat kasha next.

Nathan poked some money through the gap in the barbed wire. "Thank you, Krystia. Anything you can get, you know we're grateful for. And we saved some of what you brought us the last time, for Chanukah."

• • •

The Commandant had a different plan for Chanukah. He announced that unproductive Jews were to be sent to a labor camp. He claimed this was to alleviate the food shortage and typhus risk in our town.

On December 16, the second day of Chanukah, the gates of the ghetto were opened and police swarmed in. They brought out more than a hundred screaming, weeping people, mostly toddlers and older women. They were loaded onto horse-drawn wagons and surrounded by gun-wielding police. We watched in despair as those wagons passed down our street and out of town. How could any of them possibly escape? The hacksaws were useless against all those armed police.

I searched each face as the wagons drove by, but couldn't see Nathan or Dolik or Leon. But Mrs. Segal was on the last wagon. She sat still and dignified, clutching her cane as she was driven past the house where she used to live.

Our friends were not taken to a work camp. They were not deported. They were shot dead just a few kilometers out of town.

CHAPTER TWENTY
EATING HAY

Mrs. Segal's death made me even more determined to do everything I could to help the rest of her family live.

Mama made another trip to Lviv just as 1942 began. She had hoped to sell the rest of the stockings, as we had no food left. The chickens had stopped laying eggs in the cold weather, the tin of pork from Frau Schneider was long gone, and so were our precious jams and pickles. Maria and I worried about Mama, but we also waited in anticipation. Would she bring more buckwheat kasha? Maybe something better?

But when she returned two nights later, her face was black with bruises. Her coat was ripped and her pockets were empty.

"I had sold all the stockings," she said, "and I was coming home with salt pork, biscuits, and cash. But I was robbed on the train." She slumped down into a kitchen chair.

I held a cool cloth to Mama's face and Maria made her linden tea. We tried to comfort her, but all three of us felt defeated. That food was supposed to get us through the rest of the winter. What could we possibly do now? There was nothing else to sell and nothing we could barter for food. All we had to live on was the daily ration of one piece of bread, and water from the pump.

Auntie Polina visited a few days after that, her body so weak that she leaned heavily on a walking stick. It must have been sheer strength of will that got her to our doorstep. As we gathered close to the warmth of the wood stove, she reached into the depths of her pocket and brought out a dry wedge of cheese the size of her palm. "This is all I can spare," she said. "It will be hard for you to get through the next few months, and for me as well."

"Let us hope and pray that we all survive until spring," said Mama. "Is Krasa in good health?"

"She is," said Auntie Polina. "And Lysa is with calf as well. We just need to hold on for a few months. There will be greens and berries in the spring. And lots of milk."

But as bad as it was for us, it was worse in the ghetto. I had seen with my own eyes how crowded the Jews were. Dolik had told me that the only way to get extra food, besides what I got to them, was to buy it from the *Judenrat*, and the prices were steep. Many of the Jews were far too poor to pay for a room or extra food to supplement their daily slice of bread. Many had already starved or frozen to death. I dreaded hearing the squeaking wheels of the corpse collector's wagon, taking the dead out of town to a burial pit.

Mama cut our wedge of cheese in half, and I took one piece to the ghetto at the appointed time. It was Dolik who met me in the moonlight, and much as I was glad to see him, to know that he was still alive, my heart ached at the raspy tremor of his voice. The barbed wire had been fastened back down, so I tossed the cheese over the top of the fencing.

He caught it and slipped it into his coat pocket. "Thank you, Krystia."

"I don't know how we'll make it through the winter, and I won't be able to bring you any more food until spring." I didn't want to cry, but I couldn't help it. I felt as if I carried the weight of the world on my shoulders. I was desperate to help my friends, but at this point I could barely help myself. The whole situation was utterly hopeless.

"Krystia, take this," said Dolik, shoving a few coins through a gap in the barbed wire. "Maybe you can buy some food from the Nazis. You need to eat too."

It made me feel guilty to take his money, but I knew he was right. "Thank you," I said, putting the coins in my pocket. And as I did, I remembered what else I had to give him. I drew the latest forged documents out of my coat and poked them through to him. I also gave him a vial of painkillers from his mother's box of medicines.

"This is good, Krystia," he said. He drew a roll of undeveloped film out of his pocket and passed it to me.

I was about to leave, but Dolik said, "When you come next, can you bring sulfa from Mami's medicine box?"

"Yes," I said. "What does it look like?"

"It's a powder in red tins," he said. "Bring as much as you can carry."

"I will."

Just before I left, I held my hand flat against the barbed wire. He did the same. Our fingers and palms touched.

"Be safe," I said.

"You too."

Our entire exchange had taken less than two minutes. I hurried back across the street before the policeman finished his route. I silently darted from one building to the next on cold bare feet.

But a few steps away from our front door, a familiar voice said, "Krystia, what are you doing out?"

It was our next-door neighbor Petro Zhuk, the policeman.

"Morning chores," I said.

His flashlight pierced the darkness for one brief moment. "Chores?" he asked, directing the light at my empty hands.

Petro was no Nazi, but still, the Commandant was his boss. His job was to look for smugglers and food hoarders. Thank goodness I was no longer carrying the cheese. But if he found the film I would be in trouble.

"I was just going inside." I took a step toward the house.

"Krystia," he said, "you know I can't make an exception just because we're neighbors. Raise your arms."

His hands moved down the front of my coat and over my skirt, pausing when they reached the roll of film that was shoved in the pocket of my skirt. I took measured breaths and willed my heart to stop its wild pounding.

The silence between us hung in the air.

Then he said, "You can go now. But please realize that if the Nazis knew what you were doing, you would be shot. And if they thought that I was bending rules for you, *I* would be shot."

I murmured, "Thank you, Petro." Then I turned and walked to my front door as Petro continued on his beat. Once the door closed behind me, my knees turned to jelly and I collapsed.

Even if Mama hadn't been robbed on the train, we still would have been hungry, because the police often went from door to door and ransacked houses, looking for hidden food. They found the rest of Doctor Mina's medicines and took them away. Thank goodness this happened after I had delivered the sulfa.

They miraculously didn't find the coins from Dolik, which I had hidden beneath a loose floorboard in the outhouse.

I helped Maria fetch the water each morning, as she was too weak to carry the bucket on her own. Neither Mama nor I could work at the Commandant's any longer, because Frau Hermann said the sight of our gaunt faces ruined her appetite. In so many ways I was glad not to have to go there anymore, but it also meant that we couldn't listen in on conversations.

I was so hungry that I would go up to the loft and scour through Yasna's hay, looking for stray seeds. Mama, Maria, and I slept a lot, because with such extreme hunger, it was hard to keep awake.

We would have loved to buy some food with the money that Dolik had given us, but there was no one to buy it from because the Commandant had stopped the Volksdeutsche from selling to locals.

It had also become more difficult to do the document exchanges through the barbed wire because the police had increased their watch. I had to time it just perfectly.

Most days Maria and I walked Yasna just a few blocks down the street, then turned and came home and went to bed. At least in winter there were fewer chores. We couldn't have done them anyway.

By late February, we were like walking skeletons. Mama bundled herself up in her winter jacket and took the coins with her to Lviv. "Don't worry if I don't come home for a day or two," she told us.

Maria and I drank hot water and linden tea, trying to trick our stomachs into thinking we were full. And we went to the loft and chewed on hay.

When Mama came home, Uncle Ivan was with her. He was so thin and pale that I knew there was no more food for those in the forest than we had in our house.

"Dear nieces," he said, enclosing us both in a bear hug. "First, I want to pass on your Auntie Iryna's greetings. She sends you her love. Second," he said, "we'll *all* be eating soon."

Confused, I looked from his face to Mama's.

She smiled sadly. "Let us sit, daughters. You know that Krasa will soon give birth, and once that happens, she'll come back to us and we'll have milk."

"What about her calf?" asked Maria.

"It will stay with Polina until after the war, along with Iryna's calf and cow, because if we're caught with two cows, one will be taken away."

"When is Yasna going back to the country?"

"I just bought her from Polina with the money from Dolik."

"But she doesn't have milk," I said. "So why would you want her?"

"Nieces," said Uncle Ivan gently, "that's why I've come here today. I will be helping your mother to slaughter Yasna. With Yasna's meat, we won't starve."

I sat there, stunned. I knew, deep down, that Uncle and Mama were right. Yasna was a farm animal, not our pet, and slaughtering her for meat meant that we might survive the winter. But that didn't mean I felt good about it.

The gruesome job had to be done without the Commandant knowing, and that was easier said than done. But Uncle Ivan managed to get the carcass cut into pieces and wrapped in paper. Then we realized we had far too many packages of meat to easily hide. Uncle Ivan took some to his bunker in the forest, Auntie Polina came and took some to the country, and we filled the shelves in the coldest corner of our root cellar.

Hiding meat in my clothing to take it to the ghetto was a difficult challenge. No matter where I put it, the bulge was obvious. Maria finally tried stitching the package into the bottom of my skirt.

"But this doesn't hide the meat at all," I said, looking down at the bulge.

Maria got our second skirt and handed it to me. "Put this over top of the first one."

I did what she said and the bundle was hidden. I just had to be careful how I walked. Thankfully, I got all the way to the ghetto without incident and threw the package over the barbed wire to Nathan.

"Say hello to Maria from me," he said. "Tell her I miss talking to her."

It wasn't until after we had distributed the meat and hidden the rest that we dared to cook some for ourselves. When we sat down to that first roast beef dinner, my eyes filled with tears. "Dear Yasna," I whispered under my breath, "thank you for saving our lives and the lives of our friends."

And much as I thought I would feel awful about it, that first mouthful of beef tasted heavenly.

A few days after that first beef dinner, Marga blocked our way as Maria and I were carrying water home.

"I know about the cow," she said.

I pretended to not understand. "But Marga, I already apologized to your mother about the cow."

"Not *that* one," she said. "The old one you've had in your barn all winter . . . and now it's beef. I'm going to tell the Commandant."

We tried to step away without responding, but she grabbed my arm. "If you're so hungry," she said, "why don't you go to Germany instead of breaking the law? You could be a guest worker of the Germans. They would feed you."

I pushed her arm away and we hurried home.

"What do you think of her suggestion?" Maria asked. "Maybe if one of us left for Germany, it would be easier on Mama."

"Do you really think the Nazis treat any Slavs or Jews fairly? We'd be *slave* workers, not guest workers," I said. "Don't believe anything Marga tells you."

When we got home, we told Mama about Marga's threat.

"She may not be the only one who knows about the beef," said Mama. "Someone likely smelled it as we were roasting it. We need to hide what's left in a better place."

"But there *is* no better place," I said.

"Yes, our neighbors are all German now, so they won't help us," said Mama. "And we can't ask the Zhuks, since Petro is with the police."

"What about Father Andrij and Anya?" I asked.

Mama's eyebrows rose at the suggestion. "That might work," she said. "I'll ask."

Early the next morning, before first light, we loaded up the cart with meat and waited until the policeman who patrolled our own street had passed, then took the cart across the road to the priest.

"We won't put it in our root cellar," said Anya. "If they search, that's the first place they'd look."

She and Father Andrij hid the meat in the church's crypt instead. Hundreds of years ago, that's where parishioners had been buried. I'd also heard that in ancient times, parishioners would hide in the crypt to avoid being caught by attacking armies. It seemed somehow appropriate to hide food there to help us survive the Nazis.

And we had acted just in time. The next morning, the Commandant himself came to our door, and he brought his police.

The moment Mama opened the door he stepped in and surveyed the room, sniffing the air—probably for the scent of roast beef.

"So you've slaughtered your cow," he said.

"We did not," said Mama.

"But she is not in your shed," said the Commandant. "I've already checked."

"She's in the country," said Mama. "Where there's more hay."

The Commandant motioned to the policemen. "Check the whole house," he said.

We three stood there as the policemen went through all of our cupboards, and the loft, then went outside to check the root cellar.

They came back a few minutes later. "There's nothing here."

The Commandant looked at Mama, then at me and Maria. "I still think you're lying," he said. "You're fined twelve hundred zloty. Pay it before the end of March or I will force you all out of this house."

He slammed the door behind him.

Mama had no choice. Night after night she had to sneak onto the train to Lviv with packages of meat bound to her body under bulky clothing. She stood at the back entrance to fancy restaurants and sold each piece. It took nearly all of our remaining meat to pay the fine. But Yasna saved us from starvation. I hoped the rich Nazis who ate in those fancy restaurants would *choke* on Yasna.

CHAPTER TWENTY-ONE
AKTION

In the first days of spring, the police poured into the ghetto once again. This time they rounded up young people. Leon and Dolik both managed to evade them, but as the Nazis' wagons trundled away, I saw Nathan inside one.

It seemed that whether you could work or not, whether you were young or old, poor or rich—all Jews were targeted.

There was no question any longer what the Nazis were up to, or what they meant when they talked about an upcoming *Aktion*: Every Jew in the ghetto was slated for death.

I was sick at the thought of all these young people being shot, but Nathan was like family. We had gone to school together. We were neighbors, and he was Maria's closest friend. As the wagon he was in rolled past us, Mama and I had to hold on to Maria so she wouldn't run after him.

But two mornings after this *Aktion* we found Nathan, wrapped in a blanket, curled up asleep on our kitchen floor.

"Nathan," cried Maria. "Thank God you're alive."

He jolted awake, and for a moment he seemed not to know where he was. Maria rushed over and helped him sit up. "How did you escape?"

"They took us into the woods," he said, clutching the blanket around him. "A burial pit was already dug and we were ordered to line up in front of it and remove our clothing. But before we were even finished, they began to shoot. When the person beside me was shot and fell into the pit, I stumbled and fell in after him. I lay very still as the Volksdeutsche covered us with shovelfuls of dirt. After they left, I climbed out and ran. All I had on was my underwear. The rest of our clothing was gone. This blanket—I found it in a farmer's barn."

"We've still got some men's clothing here from Auntie Iryna's," I said. "I'll get it for you."

When I came back with what clothing I could find, Maria was sitting on the floor beside him, her arms wrapped around his shoulders. Mama handed him a cup of tea. "What are you going to do now?" asked Mama.

"If they find me here, they'll shoot me. And they may shoot you," said Nathan, shivering as he took a sip from the steaming cup. "So I can't stay here. But I'm *not* going back to the ghetto now that I'm out. Not even with Tate still there."

Nothing more was said about it that day. Nathan knew that every minute he stayed increased the risk for all of us. Mama and I went about our usual chores, as much as we could, but I noticed that Maria spent every spare minute with Nathan.

They'd sit in a corner together, holding hands. Sometimes I'd notice them sharing animated whispers, but I didn't hear what they were talking about.

The next morning when Mama and I returned from getting water, Maria and Nathan were both gone. A note was on the table:

> *We're escaping together. Pray for our safety.*
> *Love, Maria and Bohdan*

Bohdan? At first I was confused, but then I realized that Nathan must have had the passport that identified him as Bohdan Sawchuk hidden in his underwear. But where could they escape to? Would they hide on a freight train? Or maybe go into the forest with the insurgents; Maria knew the code to get through.

Mama was beside herself. "How could Maria run off like this?" she cried. "Please, God, let her be safe."

Maria had turned eleven only a few months ago, and Nathan was just twelve. But I realized that what we had seen, what we'd had to do . . . The war had made us grow up quickly.

"She's a smart girl, Mama."

"I want her *home*," said Mama. "She's too young to be out there."

For the next while, every minute of every day felt sad and empty without my sister, but I tried to comfort Mama. "You know how careful Maria is," I said.

That didn't comfort Mama at all, and deep down it didn't comfort me either. I'd wake up weeping in the middle of the night after dreaming Maria and Nathan had been shot and left in a ditch.

Maria had dressed in our old skirt and top on the day she left; I wondered if that was on purpose. Every time I put on the better clothes—the soft dark skirt and oxford shirt that had come from Auntie Stefa—I was reminded of Maria, on the run in her threadbare skirt.

I had always thought that Maria and I were opposites, and I always considered her timid, but escaping with Nathan was the opposite of timid.

I prayed that they wouldn't be caught and killed. That idea made me cold with fear. Every night before bed, I prayed for their safety, then cried myself to sleep.

We brought Krasa back home with us in mid-April. Her calf had beautiful black and white spots all over her back, just like her mother, and since she had been born in the spring, we named her Kvitka, "flower blossom." Lysa's calf was nearly all white, but she did have a black star shape on her forehead, so we named her Zeerka, or *star*. I would have loved to bring Kvitka back with us, but it just wasn't possible.

The Commandant eased up on the food confiscations now that milk was more available. A portion of our milk was still taken, but we were allowed to sell some of it, and Herr Zimmer became one of our customers. We had enough left over to make cheese.

With the warmer weather, our chickens began laying eggs again, and I could pick wild greens when I took Krasa to pasture. We didn't have a lot of food, but at least now Mama and I were no longer starving. And I continued to sneak food to the ghetto.

It was up to just Mama and me to do all our chores, and each time I carried a bucket of water home, I thought of Maria. *What is she doing now? Is she safe? And what about Nathan? Will he be able to pass himself off as a Ukrainian?* I understood why Maria had gone with him. She loved him, yes, and she wanted to protect him, but it made me feel guilty. Why hadn't I done a better job of protecting my little sister?

Mr. Segal was the only one left in his family now, and when it was his turn to meet me at our rendezvous point, he would ask if we'd heard anything about Nathan and Maria. I couldn't help but notice how much he had aged.

As spring turned to summer, the aches of mourning and loss were dulled by the busy routine of tending our house and garden and cow and chickens. Weeks went by without the Commandant issuing new notices or singling out more Jews.

Once, when we had a large batch of fresh cheese, Mama hid on the freight train to Lviv to sell it to one of the fancy restaurants where she had struck up a friendship with the chef. When she got home, she wrapped her arms around my shoulders and hugged me with all her might. "Thank God you're safe, Krystia. I heard some awful things while I was there," she said.

"What sorts of things?"

"The chef was so happy with our cheese that he had me sit in a dark corner of the restaurant and he served me a bowl of soup with a bun. As I was sipping my soup, I overheard some Nazis talking at a nearby table. They were congratulating one another on the success of their latest project to resolve the Jewish Question."

"What was their project?"

"They've completed something they called a death camp just outside the town of Belzec, a hundred kilometers from Lviv," she said.

"A *death* camp?"

"From the snippets of conversation that I heard, it sounds as if Jews will be taken to Belzec by train . . ." She couldn't seem to finish her sentence.

"What, Mama?"

". . . and gassed to death upon arrival."

"*Gassed* to death?" Mama's words shocked me to the core. "What does that even mean? And whatever it does, those men were *celebrating* this?"

I collapsed in Mama's arms and we wept.

I urgently needed to tell our Jewish friends about this new plan, but the Commandant had recently ordered even more police to patrol the ghetto, so I had to time my rendezvous perfectly.

When I next managed to get to the barbed wire, it was Doctor Mina who met me. I pulled four small hacksaws out of my pocket and passed them through the barbed wire.

"Why are you giving these to me?" she asked. "They won't help any of us escape from wagons."

"The Nazis are changing what they're doing," I told her. "It's going to get worse."

"Worse than it already is?" asked Doctor Mina. "The Nazis seem intent on killing all the Jews."

"They've built a death camp . . . killing with . . . *gas* . . ." The words came out in a sob.

Doctor Mina leaned her forehead against the barbed wire and closed her eyes. "What else have you heard?"

"It's near Belzec, two hundred kilometers from here. They'll be taking Jews there by train. This ghetto could be next."

Doctor Mina's eyes stayed closed, but in the moonlight I could see a tear trickle down her cheek. "The evil of these people never ends."

"I wish there was more that I could do to help," I said.

Doctor Mina opened her eyes and her gaze met mine. "You're a brave girl, Krystia. I appreciate everything you've been able to do for us." She looked down at the hacksaws in her hand. "Thank you for these," she said. "Maybe they'll make a difference."

"You shouldn't wait for one of those trains to Belzec, Doctor Mina. You and Dolik and Leon must escape *now*," I said.

She nodded. "You're right, Krystia. Now the ghetto is probably the least safe place. We need to escape soon, but the timing will have to be just right."

I was glad that Doctor Mina had finally agreed to escape, but how would she know when the timing was right? And where could they go to?

Weeks went by with nothing happening. Could Mama have misheard what those Nazis said? Maybe Belzec didn't really exist. Maybe the ghetto *was* the safest place to be.

More weeks went by without raids into the ghetto.

I was lulled into a routine of doing our daily chores, sneaking food and documents in when I could, and generally trying not to get noticed by the Nazis. Weeks stretched into months. But then in late July, the police stormed the ghetto.

Mama and I stood, numb with horror, as we watched them push forward a mother holding her screaming baby, and an elderly man bent over his cane. One young father held a toddler in his arms and gripped the hand of a slightly older boy. A policeman stood behind, nudging him forward with the tip of his rifle. There had to be a hundred or more men, women, and children forced into cars at the train platform.

"So this death camp in Belzec really does exist," Mama whispered. We watched, stunned, as the train chugged slowly away. The faces of terrified Jews stared out of every window.

I did not see Doctor Mina or Dolik or Leon. I could only pray they were not among these doomed people. But from one of the windows, Mr. Segal's eyes met mine.

I felt helpless. And angry.

CHAPTER TWENTY-TWO
A VISITOR

For days after that mass roundup, extra police continued to be stationed around the ghetto. I didn't dare go there for fear of being caught. I felt like such a traitor to my friends.

But then in the wee hours of the morning, about four days after that train had taken the hundred Jews, our front door squeaked open.

I scrambled out of bed.

Mama grabbed her pistol. "Stand behind me," she whispered as she quietly pushed open the bedroom door and peered out into the blackness of the kitchen.

"Kataryna, Krystia, it's me."

Mr. Segal's voice!

Mama put the pistol down and we quickly got dressed, then walked out to the kitchen. In the darkness we could make out Mr. Segal at our kitchen table.

"Michael! Thank God! How did you escape?" asked Mama.

"With this." He held up one of the tiny hacksaws. "I sawed through the window bolt and shimmied out of the train car. A few of us made it out."

"What about the Kitais?" I asked. "Were any of them on that train?"

Mr. Segal shook his head. "As far as I know, Dolik and Leon are both still in the ghetto. So is Doctor Mina."

"Thank goodness," said Mama, sagging down in her chair. "But what are you going to do now?" she asked.

"Could you . . ." He drew a deep breath. "Could you please hide me?" he asked. "I know it puts you at risk. But I can't go back to the ghetto. I was *selected* for that train. If I'm discovered there, the Nazis will kill me. But that's not what really terrifies me. They'll also select others, even hundreds of Jews, as punishment for my escape."

"Collective responsibility," said Mama. "Ivan told me of a village that was burned to the ground because of one Nazi officer being killed."

"Why were the Nazis after you in particular?" I asked.

"Forged documents were found in my coat."

"If you stay here," said Mama, "they *will* find you."

"I've been thinking about that, Kataryna. There is a way to make a hiding spot that they wouldn't find," said

Mr. Segal. "Your house is the same layout as our old house." He gestured to our wood stove. "Beneath the metal sheet under your stove is solid earth. A hiding spot could be dug in there. The metal sheet would fit on top."

Mama said nothing for a long moment. She closed her eyes. I think she was praying, because I could see her lips moving. One tear rolled down her left cheek. She opened her eyes and brushed away the tear. "I need to speak to Krystia in private," she said. "This is a decision that we need to make together."

Mr. Segal stood up. "Do you want me to leave?"

"Stay here," said Mama. "We'll talk in the bedroom."

Mama put her arm gently around my shoulders and guided me back into the bedroom. She closed the door and we sat side by side on her bed. "Tell me truthfully, Krystia. What do you think we should do?"

"It's a horrible thing to have to decide," I said, leaning my head on her shoulder. "If we don't do this, Mr. Segal will die . . . and so will many Jews who will be punished with him."

"But if we're caught, the Nazis will kill Mr. Segal, and might also kill us," said Mama.

"Would they kill *just us*?" I asked. "What about this

184

'collective responsibility'? Who else might they kill in retaliation for our actions?"

"Sometimes they'll kill families of people who have killed a Nazi officer," said Mama. "I don't know if they do that for hiding Jews."

But who was *left* to kill in our family? Maria had escaped; my cousins and Uncle Roman had already been killed. And Auntie Polina was Auntie Iryna's distant cousin by marriage, so not really family at all. I only had two relatives left who were at risk.

I raised my head from Mama's shoulder and said, "Auntie Iryna and Uncle Ivan . . . would they be punished if we're caught hiding Mr. Segal?"

Mama's eyes narrowed. "Your aunt and uncle have been risking their lives, defying the Nazis, all along."

I realized the truth of Mama's words. And it wasn't just Auntie Iryna and Uncle Ivan. Borys had defied them as well. And in our own ways, Mama, Maria, and I had been defying them too.

"I think we should hide Mr. Segal." My heart was pounding at the thought of this huge decision.

Mama leaned her head against mine. "If we do this, you must live with Auntie Polina for a while."

In my mind I saw my parents' wedding photograph.

Tato wasn't here to protect Mama anymore, but *I* was, and I would never abandon her. "I'm not leaving," I said in a voice that I hoped sounded firm. "Besides, it would raise suspicions if you were living here on your own."

"You are a brave girl," said Mama. "I'm proud of you."

We sat on the bed together in silence, letting the magnitude of our decision sink in. Then Mama said, "We should tell Mr. Segal."

"One more thing," I said. "If we dig a hole for Mr. Segal, can we make it big enough for Dolik, Leon, and Doctor Mina?"

Mama reached out and grabbed my hand. She gave it a firm squeeze. "Since they will kill us for hiding one Jew, we may as well hide four."

We walked back to the kitchen.

"We will do this, Michael," Mama said. "But we'd also like to hide the Kitais."

Mr. Segal's shoulders shook with emotion at Mama's words. It took him a moment to find his voice. "Thank you," he said.

"Can you give me three days to prepare the hiding place?" asked Mama. "Meanwhile, you need to disappear."

Mr. Segal slipped out.

The next morning, Mama went to find Uncle Ivan to help dig the hiding place.

It is not an easy thing to dig a hole in the floor of your kitchen without enemy soldiers and enemy neighbors noticing the extra activity and all the new dirt. It was hard-packed clay under the stove, and even Uncle Ivan was covered in sweat from the effort of chipping away at it.

The Nazis were on the lookout for fresh piles of dirt because they knew that there would be townspeople who would risk the danger in order to save their longtime friends and neighbors. My job was to fill my pockets with dirt and then go outside to dispose of it. Krasa's manure pile hid most of the dirt, but I also sprinkled it into the garden and onto the ground and then walked on it so it blended in. I got rid of more in Krasa's pasture, and still more in the graveyard behind our church.

But it was a *lot* of dirt.

Uncle Ivan rigged the hiding hole in such a way that between Mama and me together, we could push the stove and metal plate over to one side a bit, to make a big enough opening for Doctor Mina, Mr. Segal, Dolik, and Leon to climb into it. He also made sure to leave a gap behind the stove so they'd be able to get fresh air while they were hiding.

We put straw down on the bare dirt floor, and a

blanket over the top of that, then pillows. It looked like a horrible place to stay. I could only imagine how awful it would be with four people crowded in and the stove on top of it.

Mr. Segal came back to us three days later.

"We haven't been able to tell the Kitais of our plan yet," Mama told him.

Mr. Segal stayed down in the hole for the entire day and into the night. Once it was dark out, Mama and I pushed the stove to the side so he could get out. He gulped in the fresh air, then collapsed onto a kitchen chair. Mama gave him some milk and a bowl of kasha.

"It must be awful down there," I said as I watched him eat.

"Right now," he said, smiling sadly, "for a Jew, that hole is the best place in Lebhaft."

I had not been able to get over to the barbed-wire fence since Mr. Segal had come to our house. Word of the Belzec death camp had spread, and many Jews were trying to escape. The Commandant dramatically reinforced the ghetto patrol.

The closest I got was across the street from the ghetto. I could see Dolik standing there, but with the police passing about once a minute now, even if I got across, there wouldn't be enough time to explain our plan. So the next night I brought a written note and timed my crossing to the one-minute gap. I shoved it through the barbed wire, then immediately walked away without saying a word. Two nights later, Dolik and Leon managed to sneak out of the ghetto and reach our house.

"But where's your mother?" I asked when they arrived.

"Mami is staying in the ghetto," said Dolik, his voice faltering. "We couldn't convince her to leave her patients."

CHAPTER TWENTY-THREE
REMI

It made me proud, the act of defiance that we kept from the Commandant. Sometimes, I thought I would burst from the secret. It felt strange to carry on with our usual chores as if enemies didn't live all around us. And as if no one lived under our kitchen floor.

To divert suspicion, Mama asked Frau Hermann to hire her back—and she did. But Mama's hours were briefer and she mainly did the laundry. "I prefer that," Mama told me. "Because now I rarely encounter that evil man."

The people who had been given the Kitais' old house began buying our milk. Frau Lange was the gymnastics instructor at the school for Germans and Herr Lange worked as a town administrator. They seemed like intelligent and cultured people and they brought with them cases and cases of books, most in German, but some in other languages too. They also had a wireless radio. Most of the time they would listen to music, but I was able to overhear some of what was happening in the war, which in August was mostly about the German army heading toward Stalingrad.

Frau Lange was about six months pregnant, and now that her stomach bulged out, the principal felt it would be indecent for her to work at the school come September. I would go over to their house for about two hours a day to help her get things in order for when the baby arrived. Day by day, Doctor Mina's old medical office was slowly transforming itself into the baby's nursery. Frau Lange had particular taste and only chose the best for her new baby, but as each item arrived—the cherrywood bassinet, the ebony chest of drawers with a marble top—I wondered where it had come from. Were the old owners now in a slave camp or ghetto? Or had they already been killed? Frau Lange seemed cheerful and oblivious, and I held my tongue. But my stomach felt tied up in knots whenever I was in the Lange house. How could they seem so normal, even almost nice, yet live like vultures—benefiting from the destruction of others?

I tried to keep the bigger goal in mind. This job would help me escape notice. If I were working for Nazis, who would suspect that I was hiding Jews? But the other reason I took the job and Mama took hers was that we were feeding five people. We had to buy food to supplement what we could grow or gather. And we had to do this without raising suspicions.

One good thing about starving for so many months was that our stomachs had shrunk, and not just mine and Mama's, but Mr. Segal's, Dolik's, and Leon's. That meant that the five of us could feel quite full on the portions eaten by one or two Germans. And Frau Lange took such a liking to me that she used her influence in the Volksdeutsche store to buy extra rations. These she would give to me as my pay instead of money.

Every day as I went through my chores, I thought of Dolik, Leon, and Mr. Segal crammed together in the darkness under our kitchen floor. Did they ever panic, wanting to thrash around their arms and legs? I didn't want to ask them, because maybe thinking about it would make it worse for them. But if it were me down there, I'd want to scream. I couldn't imagine how awful it must be, cooped up like that for all the daylight hours.

In some ways it was probably better that Doctor Mina hadn't come, because there was barely room for three people under our floor, let alone four. And it made me wonder whether Doctor Mina's seemingly harsh decision was really made to keep her sons more comfortable and safe.

My favorite time those days was after dark, when Mama and I pushed the heavy stove to the side so our friends could squeeze out. Leon usually climbed out first, and I'd grab on to his arms so he wouldn't fall; he was so stiff and weak from not moving all day. Dolik was next, and then Mr. Segal. Once they were out, we'd push the stove back into place. That way, if someone came unexpectedly, the three could hide under the bed, or climb out the bedroom window and go to the root cellar or into the shed, or hide behind the manure pile.

After they had a chance to walk around our kitchen to get the kinks out, we would eat together. Things had to stay tidy, so that we wouldn't be scrambling to put away any telltale extra dishes if someone came to the door unexpectedly.

After we ate, Mama and Mr. Segal would sit at one end of the table, talking quietly about the war and any news that Mama had been able to gather or the things that I had heard on the wireless. On rare occasions, Uncle Ivan or Auntie Iryna would come by, and then the whispers got even more intense.

Dolik and Leon and I played cards, usually a game called Remi, which Leon often won. Then I'd tease him. "Remember when you used to follow Maria around like a puppy?"

"I did not," Leon protested. "I was just trying to help her."

"Better a puppy than being mean," said Dolik.

"Who are you accusing of being mean?" I asked.

"You, and you know it," he said. "It was like you couldn't stand the sight of me."

It seemed like a lifetime ago when I had been so aggravated by Dolik. Now he was my best friend. "Do you want to know the truth of it?" I asked him.

"You were jealous of me?" asked Dolik, grinning.

"I was. But not so much because you had shoes and nice clothing. I was jealous because you had a father and I didn't."

Dolik blinked in surprise, then picked up the deck of cards and shuffled them. I could tell that he was doing his best not to weep. "I hadn't thought of that, Krystia," he finally said. "And unfortunately, now we're even."

One night, to pass the time, I gathered up all our family photos and shared them with Dolik. We didn't have many, but there was one of Mama and her siblings as children—Stefa, Kataryna, and Ivan all gazing at the camera with serious eyes, wearing old-fashioned clothing. Uncle Ivan was the tallest, one hand resting protectively on the shoulder of each of his sisters. Auntie Stefa and Mama looked almost like twins, except Stefa was taller.

Dolik ran his finger over the photograph. "You'd never

know it by looking at them as children that they'd all grow up to be so brave."

It must have been terrifying for Auntie Stefa to leave behind everything that she knew and travel across the ocean to start a new life. Uncle Ivan too—to defy not one invader, but two, by trying to build an army in the forests out of nothing. I had only thought of it as *scary* when Mama would sneak into Lviv to sell things on the black market, but Dolik was right—it was brave.

"Your father was brave," I said. "He was one of the first to stand up to the Commandant. And your mother too. Think of how many would die in the ghetto if she hadn't decided to stay and help."

"I wish I had photos," said Dolik. "We took some to the ghetto with us, but they're still there. I'd give anything to see my father's face again."

I got up and rooted around on our shelves, then came back with colored pencils and paper. "Your father gave these to us," I said. "Let's make portraits on your father's paper."

Dolik took a piece and held it to his face, inhaling deeply. "It still has Tate's scent."

Dolik drew an outline of his father's face and added the black-rimmed glasses and the wild hair, but then he pushed it away. "I can't do it," he said.

I pulled the paper over and added a few more details—Mr. Kitai's lips that were always a moment away from smiling. The crinkles in the corners of his eyes. His skinny neck. I passed it back to Dolik.

"You forgot his shirt collar," he said, drawing even more details.

We drew a picture of Doctor Mina. Leon put down the book he'd been reading and picked up a red pencil. "I'm drawing you," he said to Dolik. "Why don't you draw me?"

And as they drew each other, I made a portrait of Maria. Was she still alive? And what about Nathan? I wished there were some way to find out about them both.

In the evenings we embellished the portraits and made new ones. In the mornings I would put them on a high shelf underneath our family Bible.

Leon particularly enjoyed looking through the real photographs of my family. He was struck by how closely my Auntie Stefa resembled Mama. "If this war ever ends, you should find Maria, and the three of you should go to Canada and live with your Auntie Stefa," said Leon. "That would be an adventure."

"She invited us to do that," I said. "But I'd miss you and Dolik."

Leon grinned. "Maybe we'll come too."

•   •   •

With Doctor Mina still in the ghetto, I would have liked to take food to her and see how she was doing, but Dolik said that one of her old patients who was in the *Judenrat* was getting her food. "And hiding us is risky enough," he said. "You don't want to call more attention to yourself."

He had a point. There were many ways of calling attention to yourself when there were three people hidden under your floor. For example, Dolik, Leon, and Mr. Segal couldn't go to the outhouse, so they had to use a chamber pot. Which meant that Mama or I carried a brimming chamber pot to the outhouse in the darkness of night. We also went through more water and milk. If someone were carefully watching, we could be discovered.

But summer turned to fall and we continued the ruse.

The next *Aktion* took place on September 21, 1942, which was Yom Kippur. Police stormed through the ghetto again, rounding up more Jews.

The thought of witnessing people being marched at gunpoint onto the train turned my stomach, but I had to find out whether Dolik's mother lived or not.

I counted as small children stepped onto that train of death, and grandmothers shuffled in. There were two girls my age that I recognized from school; they wept as a soldier pushed them through the train doors. Two hundred doomed Jews. Before the war, Viteretz had sixteen hundred Jews. Surely the ghetto was nearly emptied by now? There couldn't be more than three hundred Jews still alive.

One single bit of grace: Doctor Mina was not among this day's doomed.

Most of those who came to watch the Jews put onto the train cars were German and Volksdeutsche workers—the people who had come to our town and been given the property of the murdered and the food of the starving. Snippets of their conversations floated in the breeze, about how soon our area would be *Judenfrei*—cleansed of Jews.

I don't know what made me more angry and sad—the words themselves, or the satisfaction of the people who spoke them.

How I wished I could help the people who were herded onto that train, which would soon be on its way to the death camp at Belzec. I searched the crowd and noticed there were some of the original Ukrainian and Polish townsfolk standing and watching as well—and most looked shocked and disgusted at what the Commandant was doing. Did some of them have Jews within their floors or hidden behind their walls? I hoped and prayed that they did.

That night, once we moved the wood stove aside and helped our friends step out of their hiding place, Dolik and Leon clung to each other, weeping with relief at the news that their mother was probably still alive. But it was a bittersweet relief. Doctor Mina might be alive, but for how long?

CHAPTER TWENTY-FOUR
UNCLE IVAN

Our double life continued, Mama and I doing daily chores and worrying about Maria. But we heard nothing.

At night we visited with Dolik, Leon, and Mr. Segal. I got by on just two or three hours of sleep. It seemed too selfish to rest instead of talking or playing cards with our guests. I knew that if the roles were reversed, I would be desperate for company after spending the entire day in cramped darkness. But the schedule took its toll, especially with just Mama and me doing the heavy work of bringing in the harvest. Sometimes I think I slept through digging potatoes and scything wheat.

The arrangement took its toll on our guests as well. While Mama and I ached from overwork, Dolik, Leon, and Mr. Segal got weak and sick because they could barely move for much of the day.

I felt most alive when we had finished playing cards

and Leon would go to a quiet corner and read a book by candlelight. That was when Dolik and I sat side by side and flipped through pictures, or just talked. I told him of my earliest memories of Tato before he got sick, of how he'd put me on his shoulders and prance around, neighing like a horse. About how a honeybee would fly through our window each morning and land on the tip of his teaspoon. He'd feed the bee a drop of Mama's berry jam.

Dolik reminisced about visiting his father's parents in the country when he was little. "Bubbe and Zayde had geese," he told me. "I tried to pat this one big white goose, but it would run away at the sight of me."

"Did they have a horse or cows too?" I asked.

"They had an old mare named Sheyn that I'm sure had been pretty at one time."

"Did you ever ride her?" I asked.

Dolik shook his head. "She was too old. I did feed her carrots, though."

He also told me stories about his *bubbe*, who was an expert mushroom hunter. "I loved going into the woods with her," he said. "What I loved even more was eating the fried mushrooms when we got back."

We had a silent agreement to talk only of happier times. It took our minds off the fact that we were living in the midst of death.

One day in early October, Uncle Ivan visited after dark. He sipped his tea in silence and regarded us all as we sat around the kitchen table. "Kataryna, I have some news," he said finally. "Nathan and Maria came to us in the forest when they escaped. They stayed with us for a few days and I gave them some lessons in survival and living on the run. They left for Lviv, hoping to blend in with the crowd and find work. I had Maria memorize the address of a woman she could leave a message with."

Mama could not seem to find her voice, so I asked, "Have you heard anything from the woman?"

"Finally, yes," said Uncle Ivan. "One of our couriers met with her in Lviv just a few days ago. Maria had left this with her." He reached into his pocket, drew out a folded piece of paper, and handed it to Mama.

She unfolded the paper and a twenty-zloty banknote fluttered onto her lap. Mama read the letter:

Mama, don't worry. Assigned to the Huber farm near Thaur in Austria. I've heard it's not a bad place. N sends love to father. Will write when we can. Love M.

Mama rested her head in her arms and wept with relief. "I wish she'd come home so I could watch over her, but at least now I know she got out of the war zone alive."

I was so relieved to hear that Maria was safe, but like Mama, I would worry until I saw her with my own eyes.

"Thank God they got out of this area safely," said Mr. Segal.

"That's why I came here as soon as I heard," said Uncle Ivan, standing up. "But I must be on my way." He enveloped Mama in a firm hug. "Stay safe, Sister," he said. And then he was gone.

CHAPTER TWENTY-FIVE
HOLY DAYS

The Commandant had a nasty way of timing *Aktions* to Jewish holy days, but the next trains to Belzec left on October 30, which was *not* a holy day. Again, Mama and I went to the square to witness who was taken, and again Doctor Mina was spared.

The next *Aktion* was during Chanukah in December. The ghetto was emptied of all its remaining inhabitants. The police tore down walls and set fire to buildings, ensuring that every single soul still remaining in the ghetto was taken. The *Judenrat* was not spared. Doctor Mina was also not spared.

She was thin and haggard, but she walked to the train with her head held high. Her eyes searched the crowd, and when she saw me, I nodded slightly, hoping to let her know that her sons were safe. She nodded back ever so slightly—enough for me to see, but imperceptible to the police who were nudging her forward.

I stood and watched as the train doors were closed and bolted from the outside. As it chugged past me, my knees gave out and I fell to the ground. Anger, helplessness, sorrow, frustration . . . a wave of emotions washed over me. Doctor Mina had devoted her life to helping others. Why did she have to die?

Strong hands gripped mine and pulled me to my feet. "You'd best be getting home, Fräulein Krystia," said a familiar voice. I looked up. The blacksmith, Herr Zimmer.

"Thank you," I said, brushing the dirt off my clothing. Then I ran back home.

Leon knew as soon as he saw my face that his mother had been taken to Belzec. "Are we . . . Are we the only Jews left in Viteretz?" he asked.

"There may be others hidden too," said Mama. "But I'm afraid there can't be many still alive."

Leon sat down heavily on a kitchen chair and cradled his head in his arms. His entire body shook with his silent weeping. Dolik sat beside his brother, but he was silent too. He stared straight ahead with a pale face; his eyes were dry. I got out a piece of paper and pencils, then sat down with them, but kept my silence.

There were no words that could possibly bring comfort to Dolik or Leon on such a horrible day. I sketched an outline of Dolik, and beside him, Leon. On one side of the boys I drew Mr. Kitai, and on the other, I outlined Doctor Mina. Behind them, I drew the house that they'd lived in for so long.

Dolik noticed what I was doing and he tugged the paper over and took the pencil from my hand. Wordlessly, he continued to add more detail. We passed it back and forth in silence for hours.

After Doctor Mina was taken to Belzec, the five of us continued to share dinner each evening, and we'd talk in whispers and pass the time playing Remi and drawing portraits on paper, but the shadow of death was never too far away.

One evening, just after our friends had come up from under the floor, there was a knock on the door.

"Hide in the bedroom," whispered Mama.

They darted out of the kitchen and softly closed the bedroom door behind them. I looked frantically around and noticed that the stove was slightly askew, so I quickly pushed it back into place as Mama opened the door. Just then I realized that there were five places set on the table. It was too late to hide the three extra plates.

Herr Zimmer stepped in, holding an empty mug.

"Frau Fediuk," he said, with a slight bow to Mama, "I'm sorry for bothering you in the evening like this, but could you spare a mug of milk?"

"Certainly," said Mama, taking his mug. As she walked to the counter to fill it up, I stood in front of the kitchen table, hoping to block Herr Zimmer's view of the place settings.

As Mama handed the mug back, I saw that her hands were shaking.

He took the mug from her and smiled. "Thank you," he said. "How much do I owe you?"

"Nothing," said Mama. "We are neighbors, after all."

"Indeed," he said. "It is our duty to watch out for our neighbors." He bowed again and backed out the door.

After he was gone, Mama collapsed onto a chair. "Do you think he saw the plates?"

"I'm not sure," I said.

But if he did, nothing came of it. The next weeks were some of the happiest times of my life.

And then in March 1943, our world fell apart.

Mama was at the pump getting water and I was at home peeling potatoes for supper. The door burst open and Commandant Hermann himself stepped in, his Luger drawn. Behind him was an armed policeman.

"You have a Jew hidden here!" he said to me. "Give him up now and I won't punish you."

"I don't have a Jew here," I told him in what I hoped was a sincere-sounding voice. It wasn't a lie: We had three, not one. But as I said the words, even to me they weren't convincing.

"Officer Weber, check that room," said the Commandant, jerking his head toward the bedroom.

From the open door I watched the policeman rip apart our feather mattresses, pillows, and comforters, then flip our beds onto their sides to look underneath. He came out of the bedroom, leaving destruction behind him, trailing a cloud of feathers. "There is no one back there, Herr Commandant," he said.

"Then go outside and check the shed, the outhouse, and the root cellar."

Officer Weber hurried to obey as the Commandant planted his black leather boots on the dirt floor and glared at me with cold blue eyes. A vein in his forehead throbbed. He removed one leather glove and shook it in front of my face. "Tell me *now* where this Jew is!"

"We aren't hiding a Jew."

He slapped me hard across the face with his glove. I gasped and he did it once more.

"There is no Jew here," I said again. He could kill me and I still would not tell him.

He punched me hard in the stomach and I doubled over. Mama burst through the door and tried to push him away from me.

The Commandant turned to her. *"You!"* he said. "I give you a safe job, and in return you hide Michael Segal? That Jew ran a counterfeit document ring in the ghetto." He raised his Luger toward Mama's face. *"Where is he?"*

Mama stood there. Silent like me.

Officer Weber returned. "Nothing," he said. "There must be a false wall or floor somewhere in here."

The Commandant said to me, "Bring me an axe."

We did have an axe in the shed, but I would not bring it to him. I was too frightened to respond. I stood as if glued to the floor.

Officer Weber must have seen the axe in our shed, because he hurried out and a few moments later came back with it. He used the wooden handle to tap all over our wall, listening for a hollow sound, then he methodically did the same for the floor.

Mama and I stood together, our arms wrapped around each other, too horrified to breathe.

When Officer Weber got close to the metal plate under the wood stove, the hollow sound was distinct. He lifted the axe to cut through the metal, but the Commandant put his hand up. "Stop," he said. "That will not work. It would be easier just to push the stove aside. That plate underneath is likely the entry to the hiding place."

They pushed on the corner of the stove together and it moved. The Commandant took the axe from Officer Weber and used it to lift up the metal plate.

Dolik stared out defiantly. Leon was hiding his face in his brother's chest.

"These are two *young people*," said the Commandant. "The girl told us you had Michael Segal."

The girl? Had Marga told the Commandant? How did she know that we were hiding Mr. Segal?

I had a fleeting hope that the Commandant would take pity on Dolik and Leon because they were young, but Officer Weber grabbed them and yanked them both out of the hole. That's when the Commandant saw Mr. Segal.

He turned to me, his face mottled. "You *lied*."

Mama tried to put herself in front of me, but the Commandant pushed her away. He hit me hard in the face with the side of his Luger and I crumpled to the floor. He shouted to Officer Weber, "Take the three Jews to the wagon."

Then he turned back to us. "Show me your hidden gold, *now*."

"We have no gold," said Mama.

"Nothing but lies come out of your mouths," he raged. "Slavs are despicable people. You wouldn't hide Jews if not for the gold." He strode over to the cupboard and opened it, then picked up our dinner plates one by one and flung them at us. We ducked and darted as the dishes smashed into hundreds of shards. He picked up our cups and glasses and flung them against the stove and walls. Tiny bits of razor-sharp pottery flew through the air.

He reached for our family Bible and threw it so hard onto the floor that the spine split in two. He grabbed the stack of family portraits that Dolik and I had drawn, looked through them briefly, then ripped them to shreds.

Mama and I ran out the door, cutting our feet on shards of pottery. I could feel the warm gush of blood running down my face from a cut on my cheek, and more blood coming from my nose.

Outside, Mr. Segal, Dolik, and Leon were sitting in the back of a horse-drawn wagon, white-faced and silent. Officer Weber stood guarding it, but he turned and pointed his gun toward us. "Stay where you are."

We stood there at gunpoint as the Commandant ransacked our house, looking for gold that didn't exist.

When he came out, his eyes still flashed with anger. A thin trickle of blood ran through one eyebrow where a shard of pottery must have hit him. "Take the Jews to the square. Put them with the others," he said to Officer Weber.

Then the Commandant grabbed Mama's elbow. "*You* are coming with me."

I followed a few steps behind them. He took Mama to the town jail. When we got inside, Commandant Hermann turned to me and snapped, "You can't go any farther."

As he pushed her through the next set of doors, Mama turned and looked at me. "I love you, Krystia. Find Maria. You are the bravest girl in the world and . . ."

The doors closed.

I waited, my eyes glued to the doors, willing them to open.

I waited for hours.

At dusk a Volksdeutsche welfare officer stepped through the doors. She seemed surprised and annoyed by my presence. "What are you doing here?" she asked. "You're getting blood all over the floor."

I looked down. My feet and legs were covered with pinpricks of blood from the dishes the Commandant had shattered. The floor was smeared with dried blood from my pacing.

"It's all over your face too," she said, frowning.

I put my hands up to my face and flinched at the pain. I could trace the rivulets of sticky blood on my cheeks and over my chin.

"Go home," said the woman.

"I'm waiting for my mother."

"She is not leaving," said the woman. "And I'm locking up. The Commandant left hours ago."

How? I wondered. I hadn't moved. He must have left by another entrance.

When I stepped out into the town square, I spotted a group of policemen guarding about thirty Jews who were clustered there.

Dolik stood among them. He raised his eyes at the sight of me. I took a few steps forward, but a policeman raised his hand and said, "Go home, girl."

I stood there, staring at his hand, which was well-scrubbed and uncalloused. Then I looked at the policeman's face. He seemed only a few years older than me. He had the faintest wisp of a blond moustache over his top lip. Did he not consider the evil he was a part of? How could he live with himself?

I looked beyond him. Leon stood beside Dolik now, their arms around each other's waists. Behind them stood Mr. Segal, a protective hand on each boy's shoulder. How I wished I could have pushed away the policeman and run to my friends. How I wished I could have saved them. I knew what their fate was. And so did they.

I could do nothing more to help them now, so I kissed the tips of my fingers and blew the kiss to Dolik. He lifted his hand as if to catch it. And then he smiled.

With wooden steps, I turned and walked back home.

Krasa's shed door yawned open; she was gone. I checked the backyard. The chickens were also gone. I stepped carefully back into the house and grabbed the broom. I swept aside the shards of pottery so I wouldn't cut my feet. Every curtain and sheet and blanket had been torn to ribbons. Everything breakable had been smashed. Our meager supply of food had been confiscated.

As I swept the ribbons of bedding and tufts of feathers into one corner, I spied a bent piece of paper and picked it up. It was the photograph that Mrs. Segal had taken of me and Mama and Maria on the day the Nazis arrived in Viteretz. We had all been so hopeful then, thinking the war was over, thinking we would have our own country. How could we ever have guessed, back then, just how evil the Nazis truly were?

The photograph was partly ripped, and a giant boot print obscured Mama's face. I brushed off the dirt as best I could and held the photograph to my heart. "Dear Mama, dear Maria, please stay safe."

I also found Mama and Tato's wedding photo, still in its frame, but with the glass smashed. A young and hopeful Mama and Tato stared out at me, their eyes filled with anticipation. I felt as if I had let them both down. "I'm sorry, Tato," I said, tracing the outline of his face with the tip of my finger. "I tried to be brave, to do what was right, but it wasn't enough."

I gathered all the ripped pieces of the hand-drawn portraits of Dolik's family that I could find, but I didn't have the heart to put them together. The tattered fragments of their faces were a vivid reminder of my failure to keep them safe.

The bed frames were still both flipped onto their sides and leaning against the wall, but when I set them down on the floor, I remembered that the mattresses were now nothing but a pile of feathers. I took my two photographs and the ripped portraits with me and walked back to the kitchen. I knelt on the floor beside the hole where my friends had lived for so many months. The policeman had even destroyed the blanket and pillows that Dolik and Leon and Mr. Segal had slept on. All that was left was straw on clay.

I climbed into the hole, still clasping the photos and drawings. I curled into a ball and wept. Somehow, I slept.

CHAPTER TWENTY-SIX
THE COMMANDANT

I awoke the next morning with chattering teeth, clutching the pictures. I put them in my pocket so they wouldn't get lost. My mind tumbled with all the things that had happened the day before. I had to get back to the jail to see if they would release Mama.

Blood was spattered all over my clothing and feet. I'd have to clean myself before I went back to the jail if I wanted to make a good impression. When the police had ransacked our house, they'd kicked the water pail over and badly dented it, but it was still able to hold water, so I grabbed it and walked to the pump.

The street was crowded and it seemed that everyone was flowing toward the town square. The thought of why they were going there turned my stomach. Would Dolik and Mr. Segal and Leon be loaded onto the train to Belzec with the last of the Jews from our town? I had witnessed the other *Aktions* only so I could find out if Doctor Mina had been selected. This was an *Aktion* that I could not witness. I wanted to remember Dolik the way I had last seen him, standing with his brother and Mr. Segal, reaching up his hand and catching the kiss that I blew to him. And smiling.

At the water pump I saw Marga, her face swollen and bruised and her eyes rimmed with red. I had a moment of pity for her, but then saw what she was wearing—a dress that used to belong to a Jewish girl in my class. "You!" I said. "Why did you tell the Commandant that we were hiding Jews?"

"Don't hate me," she said, tears running down her mottled face. "You were pumping much more water. They beat me and still I didn't tell them. But then they were going to kill Mutter if I didn't say something . . ."

Her answer took the wind out of my fury. She was weak and probably a gossip—which might have been how the rumor of our hiding Jews got started—but she probably loved her mother as much as I loved mine. What would *I* have done to save my own mother from death?

I said nothing more to Marga, just filled the pail with water and hurried back home, ignoring all the people going in the opposite direction. I cleaned myself as best I could, but there was no soap in the house and no other clothing for me to wear. The cool water felt good on my face, but I was shocked by how much blood came off on my hands.

I hadn't eaten anything since the day before, but I was too upset to be hungry, and just as well, because there was no food. I got back out onto the street and, numb, followed the flow of the people. The train platform and the jail were both in the town square. All things led to the town square.

As I got closer, I noticed an eerie silence. There was no rumbling of a train idling on the track. If there was no train, the *Aktion* couldn't be in progress. A small relief—Dolik's life would be slightly extended.

But people were heading to the town square for some reason, and as I got closer I could hear a hum of low voices. The square came into view. A wooden frame had been erected in its center. At first I thought there was a length of cloth hanging from it.

But the cloth twisted slowly in the breeze, and as it turned, I saw my mother's face.

The Commandant had hanged Mama.

I ran to Mama's body and wrapped my arms around her legs. They were cold and stiff, but I could not believe that she was dead. "Mama . . . Mama!"

Hands grabbed at me. "Get down from there, girl," snapped Officer Weber. "Your mother is dead."

He wrapped one arm around my waist and tried to yank me away. I punched and bit and screamed.

Everything went black.

I woke with a jolt and looked around, not understanding where I was. Anya hovered over me, her brow wrinkled.

I tried to sit up, but the room swirled, so I lay back down. "Mama!" I cried. "I have to help her."

"Krystia," said Anya. "Your mother is dead. She was hanged for sheltering Jews."

"No . . ." I wailed. "Please tell me it isn't true." I wrapped my arms around Anya and wept. My entire world had shattered. Tato dead, Mama dead, Maria gone. What did I have to live for anymore? My world was entirely black.

Anya held on to me and stroked my back as I wept.

"Krystia, I'm sorry to tell you, but the Commandant has also confiscated your house and belongings." She looked into my face. "But you can live here with Father Andrij and me, as long as you wish."

Her offer was kind, but I could not stay.

Losing the house seemed so trivial compared to the murder of my mother. I ran my hand over my skirt pocket. The pictures were still there. The Commandant could kill

Mama, but he couldn't take away my memory. In my heart, Mama still lived.

"Krystia," Anya murmured, "your mother was a strong and brave soul. Always putting others' needs before her own. She was so proud of you. She said you were the bravest girl in the world."

Those were the very words Mama had last said to me. Mama had died trying to save our friends, but where were they now? As far as I knew, they were still alive, yet here I was, thinking only of myself and my own sorrow. I couldn't save Mama, but could I still do something to help Dolik and Mr. Segal and Leon?

"Have the Jews been sent to Belzec?" I asked.

She shook her head. "The Commandant has taken these last ones himself. They've been marched to the Jewish graveyard."

I stumbled to my feet, nearly fainting as I did so. "I have to go."

"You need to rest," said Anya. "You've had a shock."

"Mama wouldn't want me to rest!" I ran out the door.

My mind was in a jumble and I wasn't thinking straight, but somehow I thought that if I got to the graveyard, I could convince the Commandant not to go ahead with his plan. He had killed my mother. He had sent all the other Jews to Belzec, or had them shot here. Wasn't that enough for him? The killing had to stop. For the sake of his own soul, he could not kill Dolik, Leon, or Mr. Segal. He. Could. Not.

But when I got to the graveyard, the fresh earth bulged and quivered with the corpses of the last Jews of Viteretz. All that remained was a pitiful mound of their clothing.

Commandant Hermann sat motionless on a wooden box, a Luger in hand, splattered head to toe with blood. He looked up and saw me standing there. "You want to be next, girl?"

I turned away. I walked down the road and out of town. I walked beyond my own pasture. I kept walking until I got to Auntie Iryna's pasture—and of course it wasn't hers anymore either. But I stepped through the brush and hid in the brambles behind the rock where Dolik had found Uncle Roman's body.

It seemed a lifetime ago, so much had happened in these past two years. I curled into a ball and held my knees to my chest, ignoring the thorns and burrs. I could feel the spirit of Uncle Roman wrapping me in his arms. In the depths of my heart, I heard his voice: "You are a strong girl, my dear niece. You will get through this."

I closed my eyes and waited for darkness. *Could* I survive? It would take more luck than strength. In the early hours of the morning, I unfolded my stiff, cold legs and found my way to the insurgents' hideout in the forest.

CHAPTER TWENTY-SEVEN
HOPE

I reached the perimeter of the camp before the first light of dawn. It was quiet and still, but I knew I was being watched. I didn't dare step any closer for fear of being mistaken as the enemy and shot. I gulped in a lungful of air, then carefully, clearly, did my best imitation of the falcon's *kak kak kak.*

Then I slumped beside a birch tree and waited. Maybe I slept. When I opened my eyes, there was a boy who couldn't have been more than fourteen crouched in front of me, scrutinizing my face. A rifle was slung across his back. It was not aimed at me and I took comfort in that.

"Who are you?" he asked.

"I'm Krystia Fediuk, Ivan Pidhirney's niece. Iryna Fediuk's niece."

"Why are you here?"

"My mother has just been killed. I need to see my aunt and uncle."

"What is the answer to the question?"

"Ukraine is not yet dead."

The boy nodded. "Follow me." He signaled to people I couldn't see to hold their fire. As morning light broke through, he walked me past the snipers poised in trees and hiding behind bushes. We walked into the encampment.

Uncle Ivan wept when I told him that I was the only one left of all our family and friends. "The Commandant will *pay* for this!" he said. "I don't know when or how, but I will make it happen."

I couldn't live with Uncle Ivan, because he stayed in the underground barracks with all the men, but Auntie Iryna's living space was a room carved under the side of a hill. "You'll stay with me," she said.

When my eyes adjusted to the dim shadows of her cave room I saw a mound of stolen army uniforms—many ripped, some of them stained. "Those ones need fixing," she said. "That's one of the things I'm good at."

She found an extra bedroll for me, and while the insurgents prepared for an uprising all around me, Auntie Iryna nursed me back to health one teaspoon of soup at a time. She told me that I was a survivor, as she was. And that the way to honor our family and friends was to be strong and to live and to tell their stories.

"Who will remember them if you give up?" she asked.

Auntie Iryna found the photos and the ripped-up drawings in my pocket. She made a glue of flour and water and carefully pieced the portraits back together. We hung them on the wall of our cave. I found comfort in looking at Dolik and his family. But sometimes I'd wake up weeping, wondering if the Kitais were staring down at me in judgment because I couldn't save them. On those nights it was hard to get back to sleep.

Auntie Iryna liked to look at the wedding picture of Mama and Tato—the one that Mr. Segal had taken so many years ago—before the sadness, before the war. "Look in their eyes," she said. "See the hope and joy for the future. They want that for you."

When I was stronger, she showed me the photograph of Mama and me and Maria, the one that had been taken by Mrs. Segal. I held it to my heart and wept.

"You know that Maria is alive and safe," she gently reminded me, her arm wrapped around my shoulder. "She's probably on that farm in Austria by now, with Nathan. I think you need to find her. That's what your mother would want."

"Did you know that Auntie Stefa had wanted Mama and Maria and me to go to Canada and live with her?"

"Your mother told me," Auntie Iryna replied. "She confided in me once that her biggest regret was not taking Stefa up on the offer before the war."

"She couldn't possibly have known how bad things would get here," I said.

"That's true," said Iryna. "But I think your mother would rest easy in her grave if she knew that you and Maria were with Stefa."

Iryna's words gave me pause. I closed my eyes, and an image of Auntie Stefa formed in my imagination. She looked so much like Mama, but without the sadness of loss and war. Auntie Stefa was family. She already loved us. Now she would protect us.

My little sister had been so brave, escaping with Nathan to ensure he'd survive.

But now it was *my* time to escape, to survive—and to be with Maria again.

Together we would go to Auntie Stefa. In Canada there was food. And peace.

And freedom.

Mama *would* rest easy.

"I'm going to that Austrian farm to find Maria," I told Auntie Iryna. The thought filled me with hope. "Can you teach me what you know, so I'll have the strength and skill to get there?"

"You already have the strength, Krystia. You've proven that. But the skill—that I can help you learn," said Auntie Iryna, hugging me fiercely.

AUTHOR'S NOTE

DON'T TELL THE NAZIS was inspired by the true story of Kateryna Sikorska and her daughter Krystia, who hid three Jewish friends under their kitchen floor during the Holocaust.

Krystia is now a senior citizen who lives in Canada. Her daughter, journalist and filmmaker Iryna Korpan, approached me in 2012 at a public event. She handed me a copy of her excellent documentary, *She Paid the Ultimate Price*, and explained that it was about her own mother's and grandmother's heroic actions in World War II Ukraine. She asked if I would consider writing a book about it.

After reviewing the documentary and doing some preliminary research, I agreed. I had originally planned to write this book as nonfiction, but as I got into the interviews and research, I realized that writing it that way would not do the story justice. Many of the people who lived through those times have perished. How could I interview them? How could I quote them?

But the other problem was that as I delved into the complicated events of the time, I realized that the story extended far beyond Krystia and her family.

I archived my original manuscript and started from scratch. I located memoirs and narratives of other people in the surrounding towns to create fictional characters based on composites of those real people.

However, my heroine is true to the real Krystia. Her younger sister was Maria, and her father was a blacksmith who died before the war. Her Aunt Stefa sent packages of goods, like stockings, from North America for the family to sell should the need arise.

Dolik and Leon were Krystia's next-door neighbors. Their mother was a doctor and their father ran a stationery store from the house. Photographer Michael Klar and his wife, Lida, lived across the road from Krystia. Michael Klar took the wedding photo of Krystia's parents. He and his wife are my inspiration for Mr. and Mrs. Segal.

While pasturing his cow a few kilometers outside their town, Krystia's uncle was shot and killed by a Soviet soldier. Her cousin was killed by the NKVD—his body so brutalized that the only way he could be identified was by his crooked baby finger.

Ukrainian insurgents did capture the radio station in Lviv and declare independence from the Soviets and the

Nazis. They posted flyers to this effect all over the area. These posters were quickly taken down by the Nazis, and those leaders of the independence movement who were captured were sent to concentration camps.

Krystia really did sneak food into the ghetto and spirit out photographs. Her mother and uncle worked with Ukrainian insurgents in the area to create false documents that helped save Jews. Krystia's mother also sneaked onto the train to sell goods in Lviv.

The first names of the three Jewish friends that Krystia's family hid were indeed Dolik, Leon, and Michael. The real Nathan escaped using the false document that had been provided by Krystia's family.

All the atrocities are based on documented *Aktions* in the area, orchestrated by the Nazi regime to carry out the Hunger Plan and the Holocaust.

The Commandant and his actions are inspired by a *Kriminalpolizei* officer named Willi Hermann who was personally involved in the liquidation of the Jews in the area.

Krystia's mother's fate is real, as is that of Dolik, Leon, and Michael.

But *Don't Tell the Nazis* is a novel, not nonfiction. My story is framed around these people and events.

The real-life Krystia was only eight years old in 1941, though her courageous actions were that of a mature individual. Today's readers might have difficulty understanding that someone so young could accomplish all that Krystia did. I felt that making her older would make her actions more relatable.

Maria was only seven. Dolik and Leon were older teens. For the sake of the story I made them closer in age to Krystia so they could be classmates and friends.

Krystia also had an older sister named Iryna, who was ten, but it was Krystia who took Krasa to their pasture twice a day and sneaked food and documents into the ghetto to help the Jews.

Krystia's actual town was Pidhaytsi, which means "under the wood." I've renamed it Viteretz, which means "breezy," and I've made the town much smaller. I populated my novel with composite secondary characters based on my research.

Righteous Among the Nations

Yad Vashem, the World Holocaust Remembrance Center in Israel, conveys gratitude to non-Jews who took great risks to save Jews during the Holocaust by naming them Righteous Among the Nations. Those honored with this title are listed in a database and have their names engraved in a memorial at Yad Vashem.

Those caught hiding Jews in Pidhaytsi, and in other areas of Occupied Poland that are now part of Ukraine, were treated much more harshly by the Nazis than rescuers in other parts of Europe. Ukrainians risked death not only for themselves but for their entire families. In spite of those high stakes, more than twenty-five hundred Ukrainians have been recognized as Righteous Among the Nations by Yad Vashem for their efforts in rescuing Jews during the Holocaust.

Kateryna Sikorska's family is among them.

A Note about Terms Used in This Book

German and *Nazi* are not interchangeable: *German* and *Volksdeutsche* refer to ethnicity, not political beliefs. Some Germans and Volksdeutsche who opposed the Nazis became victims too. Others were executed or sent to slave labor camps by the Soviets.

Russian and *Soviet* are not interchangeable: *Russian* refers to ethnicity, while *Soviet* refers to a geographic area controlled by the Soviet Union. The Soviet Union contained many nationalities, including Russians, Ukrainians, Poles, and Germans.

There are thousands of mass graves all over Ukraine, yet while the Soviet Union existed, the people who lived in these terrible times and witnessed what happened during both Soviet and Nazi occupations were not allowed to talk about it. With the collapse of the Soviet Union, researchers were finally able to interview eyewitnesses and begin excavating the mass graves—graves filled with victims of both the Nazi and Soviet dictatorships.

ACKNOWLEDGMENTS

I AM SO very grateful to have worked with Sandy Bogart Johnston on this novel. It was a tough and emotional ride for both of us but Sandy got me through it. Thank you, Krystia Korpan (nee Sikorska), for opening up your memory to that terrible time and reliving your pain with me. Iryna Korpan, thank you for patiently answering all my seemingly inane questions over the course of several years. Iroida Wynnyckyj and Dr. Lubomyr Luciuk, thank you both for your precise and varied research help. Appreciation to my late in-laws, Dr. John and Lidia Skrypuch, whose terrifying wartime experiences gave me context to understand Krystia's complex story. A kiss to my husband, Orest, for his patience and encouragement. And a heartfelt thank you to dear departed Orysia Tracz, whose encyclopedic knowledge of all things Ukrainian is unsurpassed. Many times while in the final stages of this novel, I reached for the phone to call her, only to realize yet again that my friend would not be there to answer. *Vichnaya Pamyat.*

ABOUT THE AUTHOR

MARSHA FORCHUK SKRYPUCH is a Ukrainian Canadian author acclaimed for her nonfiction and historical fiction, including *Making Bombs for Hitler*, *The War Below*, and *Stolen Girl*. She was awarded the Order of Princess Olha by the president of Ukraine for her writing. Marsha lives in Brantford, Ontario, and you can visit her online at calla.com.